I0460441

DEAD LINER
A ZOMBIE NOVEL

ALEX LAYBOURNE

SEVERED PRESS
Hobart Tasmania

DEAD LINER

Copyright © 2016 by Alex Laybourne
Copyright © 2016 by Severed Press

WWW.SEVEREDPRESS.COM

All rights reserved. No part of this book may be
reproduced or transmitted in any form or by any
electronic or mechanical means, including photocopying, recording or by
any information and retrieval system, without the written permission of
the publisher and author, except where permitted by law.

This novel is a work of fiction. Names, characters, places and incidents
are the product of the author's imagination, or are used fictitiously.
Any resemblance to actual events, locales or persons,
living or dead, is purely coincidental.

ISBN: 978-1-925493-79-5

All rights reserved.

CHAPTER 1

"We are green across the board, Captain," Cillian Harris spoke.

"Very good, Mr. Harris, let's take her out to sea," Captain Joe Sheen answered, giving his now-customary three-whistle salute to the port.

The bridge came to life around him as the crew busied themselves with powering up the large cruise liner. The *Ocean Princess,* a freshly-launched ship, and the first in a proposed fleet of three liners operated by El-Hal, an Arabic based consortium with more money than there were numbers for. Each ship they had planned was to be larger than the previous one. Each one a record breaker in their own way.

At three hundred and sixty-three meters in length and with a three-and-a-half-meter draught, the ship did not quite break the record for being the largest cruise liner in the world, but by far the most luxurious. Captain Sheen joined the El-Hal company specifically to pilot the *Princess*, leaving behind his long-term position as captain of the *Oasis of the Seas*. They doubled his salary, making it their opening offer. They showed no hesitation and left Joe with no need to pursue further negotiations.

At sixty years of age, Joe Sheen knew that he only had a limited number of trips left to make. Retirement loomed on the horizon of his working life like a dark shadow waiting to swallow him whole. A single man, with one ex-wife and no children, Joe did not look forward to retirement. Sure, he would be able to read more, and possibly even pen that novel he had been promising himself he would write for the past twenty years, but he liked working; keeping busy soothed him.

Joe signed the contract after the third meeting, the final one being a small excuse for him to fly into Dubai and catch some sun, but they offered and paid for his flights, and a little enjoyment in life went a long way.

His signing did come with one condition. His XO on the *Oasis* came with him. Joe had worked with Jeff Wilcox ever since the younger man joined the company, some fifteen years earlier. A rough and ready ex-Navy man, and a veteran of several ugly conflicts, his skills were second to none. His rough-around-the-edges persona did not exactly match what people expected to find in the cruise business. Joe took Jeff under his wing, and within no time, the pair formed a bond that only grew with time.

Joe understood Jeff's initial scepticism, but after one meeting with the El-Hal executives, a look at the plans for the ship and a salary that quite literally made his jaw drop, Jeff signed before the first meeting ended.

It was not the money, but rather working with Joe, which served as the key factor behind his decision, but he would not let on to the fact.

Their friendship grounded Jeff. When he left the military, he did not know where he was going to go. Joe helped him, showed him a new way of life that still resembled military life in enough dimensions to keep Jeff in place. Best buddies enjoying a friendship which at times bordered on being a father and son bond.

Being the ship's maiden voyage, the seven-day cruise sold out in remarkable time, meaning six thousand passengers boarded the ship. Each of them expecting to find something that went a cut above the other cruises out there. Something that would explain the higher than average ticket price.

They got it as soon as they entered the ship. The staff lined the gangway and greeted each passenger as they boarded, bowing their heads and shaking hands with those that offered. Inside, everything was new and state-of-the-art. From the carpet, a thick and plush shag with a vibrant and healthy maroon colour, to the walls, which were equal parts polished wood and blemish free white. Crystal glass lighting hung on the high-ceilinged entrance hall. Everything gleamed and sparkled, and you could hear the collective intake of breath as people crossed the threshold.

"How is she handling, Mr. Wilcox?" Joe asked as the boat left the docks and moved into the centre of the Dubai harbour.

"Like a dream, Captain," Jeff answered with a smile spread over his face. "She moves like a motherfucking dream in the water."

"Eloquent as always, Jeff." Joe clapped his friend on the shoulder. He gave a laugh when he saw the shocked faces on the rest of the bridge crew. The heavily Arabic crew looked over at them, clearly still taken aback by the laid-back atmosphere of the recent exchange. "Don't worry. He is an acquired taste, but you will get used to him soon enough."

Fifteen decks below them, the ships six fifteen-thousand kilowatt Wärtsilä engines growled to life, and the eight AAB Azipod bow thrusters powered down, their immediate task of moving the ship away from the dock complete.

Despite the fact that the engines boasted a combined power output greater than that of a space shuttle, the boat barely moved as they powered up.

"Let's take her out to sea and find out what she can really do." Joe stood beside his XO and watched the endless, impossibly blue ocean stretching out before them.

The weather forecasts for the coming seven days promised to be a cruise captain's dream. Nothing but fantastic, blue skies, smooth seas and temperatures hot enough to keep everybody on board happy. The ship offered more than enough attractions to keep the passengers engaged for the full seven days, and then some. For those that loved the sun, and those that loathed it. Inside and out, the *Ocean Princess* provided more entertainment than many of the towns and cities either man ever spent time in.

"This calls for a cup of coffee," Joe decreed, turning to help himself to a cup from the state of the art machine. Joe considered himself to be a coffee enthusiast, he knew good coffee, and while the make and model of the machine said nothing to him, he could not deny they made a delicious dark, rich and delicious brew.

"Like you need an excuse to have a cup of coffee," Jeff cut back with a smile.

"You want one or not?" Joe returned fire.

"Hell yes," Jeff answered, turning his eyes back to the sea. "This sure is the life, isn't it?"

CHAPTER 2

Robert Nash opened the door to his room and stood in the doorway for a moment, staring at it. He was sure a mistake had been made when assigning him his room. So sure of it, in fact, that for the first hour after he had made a phone call to the reception desk to confirm they gave him the correct key, he still found himself close to being afraid to pick up his bags and unpack.

The enormous room looked to be at least twice the size of the master bedroom in his own home. The grand king bed, at least Robert assumed it to be a grand king, for he did not know of a larger manufactured size, soon became his favourite part of the room. Even at six-feet-four, he could lie across it without having his feet or head anywhere near the edges. The dual layer mattress embraced him as he lay down. Robert imagined that lying on a cloud would feel just the same way. He could already feel the stress and anger lifting from his body after but a few moments folded in the mattress's sweet embrace. The last eighteen months had been the worst period of Robert's life. While it culminated in his high school sweetheart leaving him, serving him divorce papers on the same day he heard his department at work was going to be making cutbacks, his soul wept knowing that compared to everything else, it could not claim top spot on his list of problems. The cruise offered him the chance to find himself again. To unwind and maybe let go of the anger that had consumed him, finally getting back to being Robert Nash once more.

Aside from the bed, the entire room screamed luxury. The thick, deep navy carpet tickled gently on his bare feet; the discarded shoes lay haphazardly beside the bed. Robert brought a pair of flip-flops with him that he planned on wearing whenever footwear was required. He couldn't care less if certain areas of the ship carried a particular dress code. He paid a lot to be on board, and was going to dress his way.

The bathroom presented an equally luxurious first impression. The initial blast of light from the powerful spot-lamps in the ceiling came as a bit of a show, but once Robert got the hang of the different switch combinations, he realized it could be kept to a manageable level. The shower offered four different jet points and a short twist of the tap told him the water pressure was more than adequate for them to do their intended job.

Designer brand miniature soaps, gels, creams and pastes lined the deep-set sink. A simple ceramic tiled setting, with cream and blue being the theme of the room, even down to the shower curtains and towels.

The room also boasted a large desk with a matching chair, a coffee table and two armchair styled seating places and a wardrobe twice the size Robert would need. A large cabinet beneath the wall-mounted television featured a mini bar, which was fully stocked with everything he could think of, and unlike hotels, where you needed to either call room service or wait until the next day for the stock to be replenished, the mini bar on the *Ocean Princess* restocked itself. When the door closed, the system knew to deliver the missing goods via a series of shoots. Everything in the same place and in the same quantities, all the time.

Robert smiled as he pulled out a small bottle of Southern Comfort, closed the door, waited for the subtle *clink* of a fresh delivery, opened the door and took a second bottle. He emptied both into a glass, added some ice and slouched into one of the large armchairs. Not quite as comfortable as the bed, but a close second.

"I could get used to this," Robert said aloud to the room. He sipped his bourbon and watched the TV.

With the remote in hand, Robert meant to zap through the channels, but he found it oddly interesting watching the ship's default channel. A rotation of different scenes. A computer generated graphic of the ship pointing out its technical prowess, everything from the engines up to the radar systems and weather capabilities. The second showed a series of images taken from within the ship, highlighting the key areas, from the sun deck and multiple pools, through to the park-like gardens, aquarium and outdoor activities. In truth, the boat offered more entertainment than most cities, certainly the ones Robert had lived in during his forty-four years on the planet. The third round of information gave a shot through the fore and aft facing cameras. There were two positions from each one. One from the main passenger deck, capturing the pool and water slide on the fore-facing camera, and one from the bridge on the uppermost of the fifteen levels.

Turning in his chair, Robert pulled back the curtain that covered the large porthole window and stared out at the ocean. Deck nine, the highest cabin holding deck, unless you counted the twenty-two suites which, while based on the same deck, actually covered two, with a staircase being present inside each room, taking their occupants from the ground floor living area to the upper level sleeping quarters.

Robert finished his drink, and while sorely tempted to go back to the fridge and grab another, he forced himself to head into the ship and have a nose around. He could happily sit in the room for the whole seven days, but that would be a waste of the money he had spent. Getting dressed, deciding to skip having a shower until after he got his bearings and had a general feel for the ship, Robert left the room and headed off to explore.

CHAPTER 3

Derrick Darrow needed to swipe the card for their door four times before it opened. Not that he could blame the card, but rather the sticky mess that covered it. His daughter insisted on holding the door card, doing so in the same hand she used to eat the candy bar given to her when they boarded the boat.

"Ok, new rule. No sticky fingers on the door keys," Derrick said as he finally opened the door and stood back, allowing his wife and children the opportunity to enter first.

They had taken the large family cabin with an ocean view, despite the overall size of the room being bigger than almost all other cabins, and the two extra beds, even if they were only singles, reduced the amount of available floor space. Still, the set-up looked impressive and left the whole Darrow family speechless for a moment.

"This was definitely worth the money," Derrick said as he wrapped his arm around his wife.

"I think this is exactly what we need," Carol Darrow answered, resting her head against her husband's shoulder. She sighed when she felt him stiffen at her touch. Only a slight motion, a lot less noticeable than in recent months, but it still broke her heart just the same.

"You could be right," Derrick said, giving his wife a kiss on the top of her head. She felt the stiffness behind his lips too. Before, it would have been a kiss on her lips, and stiffness somewhere else.

Carol closed her eyes. Their therapist recommended they try a vacation as a family, but he warned Carol not to expect magic. Change took time, acceptance being just the first step. He made it very clear to them both that rebuilding a marriage could not be done in a day. Carol wanted to be angry at her husband, but in truth, she only blamed herself.

She broke their wedding vows by sleeping with not one, but several different men. Her inability to cope with the guilt only served as a trigger for her to run from bed to bed. Laying her head and spreading her legs in every bed apart from her own. She became withdrawn from her family and each time she rolled over and saw a different face staring back at her, she became further convinced that Derrick would leave her when he found out.

The day she finally broke down and told him the truth still made her feel sick. The worry and the stress made her physically ill, leaving her vomiting for days before finally finding the courage to confess. Derrick took the news without flinching. From the moment Carol finished talking, his emotions stopped, turned off by a switch inside his head.

Carol cried for days, her mood only made worse by the way Derrick continued as if nothing had changed. He got the kids ready for school and dropped them off on the way in to work, while she struggled to hold herself together long enough to get dressed and out of the house on time for her own job.

The silent treatment lasted for over a month before Carol finally cracked. While serving dinner one evening, she began to scream, and hurled the dinner plates against the wall. Derrick had suggested the idea of a meal together, organizing with the family for the kids to stay at one set of grandparents for one night, and the next with the other. Yet, he remained silent, not speaking to his wife the entire time. Derrick responded to the thrown plates and string of screamed obscenities by rising, grabbing Carol by the arms to spin her around. He then made angry love to her over the table. He fucked her in a way he never contemplated before, grunting and growling as his hips slapped against her ass cheeks, harder and harder, driving like a piston until Carol screamed out in delight.

Derrick came, dressed himself in silence, turned away and walked to bed. The next day Carol confronted him, and they fucked again, pulling the bathroom cabinet from the walls as they did. Their relationship carried along the same path for another two weeks, with them fucking in raw, angry, wordless lust at least once a day, and each time Derrick would be the aggressor, usually taking his wife from behind in some way. Carol felt dirty after it, often weeping. Derrick would shower and continue with his day, shutting down more and more.

Carol made the first move to repair things when she suggested they try therapy. She blurted it out one afternoon after their latest session in the kitchen. Derrick stared at his wife, shrugging his shoulders. "Alright," he said, uttering the first real words to his wife since the admittance of her infidelities, and the last, too, until their first therapy session.

Neither of them expected therapy to be easy, but they did not expect it to be as hard on them as it was. Most sessions ended in tears. They reconciled, and quickly got to the bottom of why Carol cheated. While there had been many long words, and even longer explanations, it boiled down to a mid-life crisis of sorts. With two kids and a dead end job that she despised, Carol had broken down and gone in search of something that made her feel young again. Sex called to her, it drove her in her thirties the same way it did in her teens.

Now, four months later, their family was whole again, although Carol knew that things could never be as they were before. She would have days when it all came rushing back to her. Moments when she would feel Derrick stiffen and pull away. He was trying, and she prayed every day in thanks for his understanding and acceptance, maybe even his forgiveness. She needed to hear her husband forgive her. Maybe then she would sleep through the night without waking either trembling, crying, or both.

"Mummy, I don't feel very well," Celia, the couple's eleven-year-old daughter, groaned. She started complaining of stomach pains as they stood in the queue to board.

"It is just nerves, darling, that's all. Let's get you a glass of water, and then maybe we can go explore a little," Derrick said, crouching down to his daughter's eye-level.

"Ok, but my throat hurts," Celia answered, her voice weaker.

Derrick crouched down and placed his palm against his daughter's forehead. "You do feel a little hot. Maybe a lie down and a nap will do you some good."

"I don't want to go to sleep." Celia's eyes went wide, an expression of pure fear etching itself onto her face.

"Why, honey?" Derrick asked. "There is nothing to worry about."

"Because I'm scared. I don't want you to leave me alone while I sleep." Celia grabbed her father's arm and squeezed it tight.

"I won't leave you. I will sit right here with you while you have a nap. When you wake up, we can go exploring. Maybe find you an ice cream for your sore throat. Come on, lie down here." Derrick patted the first single bed.

Celia didn't complain and slid beneath the covers. As an infant, Celia suffered from terrible night terrors. She would wake up screaming, and would not go back to sleep in her own room no matter what Derrick or Carol tried. As she aged, the phobia settled down, the nightmares and terrors became fewer. Neither could recall the last time their daughter had actively mentioned her fear of sleeping.

CHAPTER 4

"Would you take a look at this?" Sofia de Grassi squealed as she looked around the luxury suite that she and her boyfriend would have to themselves for the coming time.

"This is incredible," Jose Espinoza, her long-term, long-suffering partner remarked. Jose first asked Sofia out on a date in their first week of junior high. He did not care for the standard protocols of school hierarchy, or that Sofia was a year older than he was. Even back then, he was a man that knew what he wanted, and did what he needed in order to get it.

"You are worth every penny," Sofia whispered in his ear. "Happy anniversary."

Sofia kissed Jose on the cheek, brushing his medium-length black hair to one side. Her tongue darted from her mouth and traced the edge of his ear, causing Jose to shudder. Turning around, Jose pulled Sofia against him, his lips finding hers, their tongues caressing with a growing intensity, desire overflowing.

Their limbs wrapped around one another, bringing them even closer together. They stumbled through the suite, until they collapsed onto the large sofa that offered the main seating options in the lower of the two floors in their suite.

Ultimately, Sofia broke their embrace. "Slow down. I promise, these five days will be unforgettable." Sofia leaned over and bit Jose playfully on his lip, her hand brushing against his crotch.

"That's not fair," Jose began.

"Oh, you've waited this long, let's not worry about a few more hours. Don't worry, baby, I'm worth it. I promise." Sofia winked as she turned away. "I need a shower. Take a look around, and when I'm done we can explore the boat a little."

"I could join you..." Jose began.

"No, you can't." Sofia giggled, locking the door to the bathroom behind her.

Despite being together for over four years, the couple had yet to sleep together.

Sofia came from a wealthy family, a family several levels above Jose's on the social scale, and their relationship came as a surprise to both families. Sofia's father was a traditional man, and believed in the sanctity of marriage. Sofia loved her father, the only child in a family that boasted a proud heritage of spawning copious members of the next generation. As such, Sofia found herself placed under a large amount of pressure to behave, and be the prim and proper de Grassi child.

It did not help that her father was one of the world's most sought-after lawyers, having represented everybody and anybody to great success—provided they could afford his services. Constantin de Grassi came from humble beginnings, from a family of Italian immigrants. Raised by a single mother, having lost his father in the Second World War, he could only recall the faintest memories of the man. After moving through Europe, growing up in almost every country from Italy, across Austria, the Czech Republic, and Poland, through and into Scandinavia. It was there that he met the love of his life, a blonde-haired, blue-eyed Swedish beauty. Together, they moved to America with the rest of Constantin's brothers and sisters, who numbered eight in all, joining them at various intervals over the following four years.

The lovebirds waited, obeying the rules of the family, as hard as they found it on many occasions. They loved each other, and the moment Jose turned sixteen, he proposed. He saved his wages from his weekend and evening jobs at both a supermarket and a pizza parlour to buy the ring. He also used the money he planned to fund his college education. However, he justified the ring an expense he happily indulged in. He would do anything for his Sofia.

Constantine loved Jose like a son. He respected him as a young man, having also grown up without a father. Constantin approved of their marriage, but under the condition that they did not marry until they turned at least eighteen. He also stipulated, during the same family meal, that providing Jose continued to achieve the same good grades, Constantin would pay for his college education, the full package. The announcement brought Jose's mother, Maria, to tears.

By the time Sofia came out of the shower dressed in a pair of short denim shorts and light pale yellow shirt, Jose had just finished unpacking their bags, which they did not need to touch from the moment they checked in at the dock. They stood waiting for them in the room when they opened the door.

"You look amazing," Jose said with a smile, sweeping Sofia into his arms. "Especially with that on your finger."

Sofia giggled and looked down at her hand, where a simple, elegant gold band wrapped around the fourth finger on her left hand. The beautiful diamond and white gold ring made a stunning addition to Sofia's appearance. Their wedding ceremony turned into a simple affair, not the grand occasion the family seemed intent on throwing. Then again, when cancer strikes, plans are changed. The things once considered important get pushed to the back of the line. Family mattered the most to Sofia, and she wanted her father to walk her down the aisle while he still could.

The doctors gave Constantin close to a year, but they wanted to move fast. Connections and favours got cashed in. The wedding, ceremony and honeymoon was arranged and held less than four weeks after Constantin received his diagnosis. As with everything in life, he faced his illness with a stubborn aggression, and refused to allow people to be sad. The wedding turned into a celebration of life and love on a much grander scale. The honeymoon, a surprise gift to his daughter and son—for that was how Constantin addressed Jose—came with the order that they eat, drink and enjoy themselves.

"Shall we take a look around? I have heard wonderful things about this ship," Sofia said, already moving to the door before her doting husband could respond.

CHAPTER 5

Eric Brown unzipped his suitcase and let out a satisfied sigh. He had been saving his whole life to take a cruise, and while the timing could have been better, the lure of the open seas could not be resisted. Eric booked the tickets, using up his life savings to do so, and not three days later got a call offering him his dream job. They wanted him to start straight away, presenting him with an opportunity he dared not pass up. Writing for DC Comics had been his dream since he picked up his first copy of The Flash some thirty years before. When Eric mentioned the cruise, he held his breath, expecting them to snatch the offer away from him, or at best, offer him an ultimatum. His jaw nearly hit the floor when they wished him a pleasant vacation and gave him the contact details to use upon his return.

With his suitcases unpacked and his dirty clothes lying on the floor, Eric stood up straight and walked through the room and into the bathroom. He reached through the curtain and turned on the shower, impressed by the pressure generated by the showerhead.

Stepping beneath the hot stream he groaned as the water washed over him, rinsing away the sweat and dirt of travel. Eric had travelled a lot in his years, and nothing made him feel dirtier. He made it his routine to always shower as soon as possible, flushing away the grime. His skin turned red from the hot temperature of the water, but he didn't care. Coming off the back of a crazy few months, Eric needed the break in order to fully process everything.

The water washed away the stresses and the weights that had been bogging him down. As a full-time writer, Eric knew better than most what it was like to stand on the wrong side of broke. People held the wrong idea when it came to the wealth of full-time writers, thinking they all lived the lavish lifestyle of the social elite. The sad truth being, more often than not, dinners consisted of Ramen noodles and a glass of cheap soda, not to mention the international anonymity that his decent but not world-shattering sales generated. Not that he would change it for the world. He loved what he did, and while there were times that he wished he had more freedom when it came to what he wrote, he remained passionate. It was the ultimate career, the only one he saw himself doing. It could be tough, and did not naturally lend itself to prolonged bouts of relaxation, but Eric loved it.

Stepping out of the shower, Eric felt like a new man. He smiled and whistled to himself as he dressed, grabbed the top couple of comics from his bag and headed out of the door. The boat did not set sail for another couple of hours, but he didn't care. The sun shone brightly in a cloudless blue sky, and the lounge chairs were calling him. Seeing as how he spent most of his life indoors, either hunched over a keyboard or reading either comics or novels, his skin took on a horrid, pasty white complexion. Eric promised himself that if he got anything out of the cruise, a good tan would be it.

The eighth deck had a bustling quality to it, alive with activity as people wandered the halls in search of their rooms. A family moved past him; the three children came first, two boys and a girl. They charged down the hallway, their rather bedraggled-looking parents coming up behind them, pushing and pulling a mass of suitcases and bags.

Eric smiled and said hello to the couple, who looked exhausted and no doubt planned on using the coming days to relax as much as possible before the rigmarole of family life started again.

The long, wide hallway, with its thick maroon coloured carpet and cream painted walls, led to a central square where three different elevator shafts could be found. The ship had four of these units spread throughout its length. That said, the queue for them was crazy long, and rather than wait, Eric took the stairs. The carpet continued through the stairwell, with a thick brass handrail following the spiral of the main stairwell.

Eric moved up to the eleventh deck where he found a swimming pool, already bustling with enthusiastic children, and a large sun deck sporting a range of individuals that moved through every shade of the suntan rainbow. It began with a few people even whiter than him, their bodies drenched in sunscreen, before hitting the golden brown and bronzed bodies of the permanent sunbathers, and at least one rather large man who lay snoring on a recliner, several empty beer cans hidden in the shadow of his bulk. His skin so red it glistened like the raw meat inside a wound.

Picking his way through them all, Eric found a small set of steps that led to a second deck, a half deck really. It was quieter up there, with a small bar getting ready to serve those that found the hidden gem of a location. Picking a recliner, Eric deposited his things, grabbed himself a nice, strong drink, and settled down for an afternoon of reading.

The warm sun and vibrant company put Eric at ease. All around him the giggles, cries, whoops and all other possible exclamations of joy rang out as the boat's engines came to life, and they moved away from the dock.

The time flew, and before Eric realized it, two hours had gone by. Finishing the final comic that he brought from his room, he looked around. The half deck had gotten busier, but still not full. The lounger to his left was occupied by a woman of his approximate age, but it was painfully obvious that she weathered the test of time a lot better than he did. From her toned stomach to her shapely legs. Her skin was a glorious, healthy shade of brown, but far from the leathered look of a full-time sun-sloth. She wore a white bikini that hugged her large breasts and a pair of briefs that rode high on her hips, complimenting her shapely legs.

"Least you could do is buy a girl a drink," she spoke from behind her sunglasses. Her head turned toward Eric, a smile stretched across her face.

"Oh, I'm sorry, I just…" Eric stammered, caught. Heat flushed his face and he knew his cheeks had turned as red as burning embers.

"I'm just joking with you. My name is Tara." She extended arm and shook hands with Eric, who smiled and felt his blush worsen.

"Eric, Eric Brown. It's a pleasure to meet you. Could I maybe get you a drink?" Eric returned the smile he had received, and felt a wave of relief run through him when Tara did not move away.

"Thank you, that's very generous. Why don't you surprise me?" she said with a wink.

Eric returned with two drinks, and watched when Tara sipped hers and accepted his choice. He could not claim to be a drink guessing genius, but he did have the common sense to ask the bartender to make the same again for the lady.

The pair got to chatting, nothing too personal, just the standard holidaymaker chitchat. Eric liked having a little company, although he was equally comfortable when Tara rose from her lounger and said goodbye.

Eric watched her leave. She was a beautiful woman, there could be no denying that, but Eric did not come on the cruise with the intention to fall in love. Not just now.

Eric remained on the sun deck for a time, but with his reading material exhausted, and a familiar rumble growing in his stomach, he called it a day and went in search of some food.

CHAPTER 6

Robert made it back to his room before the boat pulled away from the harbour. His growing affinity for the delivery system in his mini-bar resulted in quite the happy buzz; Robert decided it high time to go in search of alcohol served in slightly larger quantities.

Ordinarily, Robert was not a drinking man, but after the last few months, he owed it to himself to indulge a little.

His brief exploration of the ship allowed him to gather his bearings. He returned quickly enough, thirsty and eager to experience and enjoy the quiet of his room. The solitude felt good for his soul.

Leaving his room again, stumbling as he walked, Robert made his way to the sports bar on deck twelve. The ship played home to seven different bars, and Robert had plans on visiting all of them at some point in time during the trip. His chosen watering hole was a sports bar with several people already placed around the tables that offered the best view of the three large screen TVs, each of which showed a different live event. Robert did not have any real interest in football, rugby or golf, and so moved straight to the bar.

"What can I get you?" the friendly voice of the bartender asked. He was a small Indian man with a well-trimmed moustache and jet-black hair, cut short and sharp.

"I'll just take a beer for now, thanks," Robert said looking around. The bar was at the front of the ship, and gave a great panoramic view of the open ocean. The bar also merged with a general seating area, which accounted for the majority of the viewing area, but with a cold beer in his hand, Robert found the draw of the view too strong.

Soft jazz music played in low tones and the quiet murmur of contented conversation created a very relaxing atmosphere. The sun, sky and sea made a hypnotic combination, and within a few minutes, Robert slid away from the world and into a state of peace.

Three beers later, and Robert was drunk. Not the paralytic, but certainly a little more than buzzed. His head spun, and for the first few seconds after he stood, he thought he would fall.

Holding onto the table until confident in his balance, Robert stumbled out of the bar and back to his cabin. He needed a shower and a nap before getting something to eat.

There was one other man in the lift when it arrived. He stood hunched over in the corner, and even in his inebriated state, Robert could sense that something was wrong with him. While Robert was drunk and needed help in keeping his balance, the stranger in the elevator looked as if he were doing everything in his power to simply remain on his feet. Sweat poured from him, dripping to the floor, bringing with it a certain odour, one of sickness.

"Are you alright?" Robert asked, concerned.

The man gave no response, but raised his head to look in Robert's general direction.

His eyes were unfocused, the whites stained pink, as if he had been weeping. Thick strands of green snot dripped from his nose, hanging from his upper lip like elastic bands. He opened his mouth and gave a gargled growl of a response.

"You really don't look too sharp. We should get you to—" Robert could not finish talking for the man gave a belch and spewed a thick, foul-smelling stream of vomit onto the floor of the descending elevator.

The force behind the projection was enough to cause the thick fluid to splash up to knee height on Robert's trousers. The man then promptly fell forward, landing face-first in the substantial pool of vomit.

The effect of the alcohol washed away on the rolling acidic stench of puke. Robert gave a groan as he crouched down and shook the man. His body was heavy, cold in spite of the fact that the man clearly burned with fever until the moment he keeled over.

"Hello?" Robert shook the man harder. "Hey, dude, wake up."

The elevator continued to move. It felt as if it took an age to drop what was, in essence, but a few floors.

Groaning as his hands slid through the cold, oatmeal-consistency vomit, Robert took hold of the man and rolled him onto his back. The man was dead, his eyes a dark shade of red, his tongue purple and bloated and black like a giant leech.

"Holy shit." Robert jumped to his feet, almost slipping as the descending cage came to a sudden stop.

The doors opened and the screams began. A family of four stood waiting for the elevator to take them to the upper decks, a drunk and a dead man being the last thing they expected to find waiting for them.

"Somebody needs to call a doctor," Robert slurred, walking out of the elevator with vomit hanging from his hands like melted skin. The two children, who could not yet have even been in double digits, began to scream and weep in alternating breaths. The mother fainted, and the father stared, catching his wife in a near-nonchalant fashion, which, under other circumstances, would have been a very smooth move.

The screams soon attracted a host of new faces to the crowd, all of whom seemed to be casting glances in Robert's direction. After all, simple deduction picked him as the killer. At some point, he did not know when, three burly-looking security officers arrived. Their dark, sweat-slicked skin paled visibly as they took in the scene before them. Sights and stenches that nobody could ever become accustomed to had all three men retching as they attempted to gain control over the crowd.

Robert stood in the elevator. They told him not to leave, and it seemed as safe a place as any to sit and await his fate.

With control restored, the guards cleared the hallway before returning to deal with the body. In spite of its size and facilities, the *Ocean Princess* did not have the required facilities to adequately house the dead, nor to transfer them through the ship. They decided to take the elevator down to the cargo hold. A simple override key allowed the passenger elevator to drop the extra levels below normal passenger access. Robert went along for the ride. The guards eyed him with suspicion, but none actually suggested they planned to detain him for anything more than taking his statement.

The cargo hold was enormous—a grand open space, half the size of the ship. Large containers stood in the dark like ruins. Far from full, it still surprised Robert that so much cargo managed to find its way onto a simple pleasure cruise.

"That's a lot of cargo. Is it filled with things for the trip?" he asked, not expecting an answer.

"No, this cargo is being delivered as we go. The space cannot be used by passengers, and while the ship is docked at a port, it is just sitting there," the third guard, the one escorting Robert, answered.

"Makes sense," Robert added, nodding.

"Makes money," the guard responded with a short, sharp guffaw.

Robert looked around as they moved. He realized the hull had been separated into two equal storage spaces, a large iron wall acting as the barrier. The dazzling yellow partition seemed to be their intended destination. The two men in front were carrying the body between them. One had the arms, while the other had the feet. The deceased's head lolled back, the still-open eyes staring at Robert and his guard as they brought up the rear. While not the most respectful way to move a body, Robert understood that needs must when the devil drives.

By the time they reached the service elevator and had ridden it back up to the third deck, where the security station and medical bay were located, Robert no longer felt anything of the alcohol he had consumed.

"You can follow me. The captain will want to have a word with you," the third guard, whose name Robert did not know, spoke.

Robert followed the man down the corridor, while the three men—two living, one dead—turned to the left at the first junction and disappeared from view.

The room was a tiny bare-walled cube, with a simple table and fold-out chairs hanging on hooks against the wall. Whoever designed the ship did not put much thought into the possibility of detainment.

The security officer left the room, and Robert sat alone waiting for the captain. His first thought conjured an image of the captain of the ship, but when a man clad in the security uniform appeared, Robert corrected himself.

"Good day, I am Captain Rasheed. I would very much like to talk with you." The man collected a chair and sat on the opposite side of the table.

Captain Rasheed looked about as far removed from the image generally associated with security guards as Robert could imagine. A small man in all ways, no taller than five-feet-six and no heavier than seventy kilograms with his boots on. His skin was a caramel colour, with short black hair and a closely-trimmed small moustache. His bright brown eyes could not stop moving, darting from one point to another.

Robert felt nervous. "I'm not under arrest or anything, right?"

Captain Rasheed gave a startled laugh. "No, no, my friend. We know you did not kill that man. We have cameras in the elevators. We can see that he was sick. I just have some questions I would like you to help me with." He fidgeted on his stool, his eyes making only the briefest of contact with Robert before flitting away to another focal point.

"I don't know what I can tell you. If you have cameras then you know everything already. I got in the elevator. I saw the man and asked if he felt alright. He didn't say anything, just sort of growled, vomited and keeled over. I tried to help him, but...but he died." Hearing the words spoken shook Robert more than he cared to admit.

He did not know the man, but at the same time, he had been there at this stranger's end. His voice was the last sound the stranger heard before dying. The weight of that knowledge pressed down on him more than he wished.

"I understand, my friend. Please, tell me, did you know this man? Had you seen him before somewhere?" Captain Rasheed asked awkwardly. The pauses added between his words were not designed to intimidate Robert, nor to make him feel the pressure, but there simply because the captain did not know what to do.

"Me, no, I've never seen the man before. I have only been on the ship a few hours. I spent them in my room and at the bar. I'm not looking for any trouble. I just want to have a good time. I am kind of celebrating, you see."

"Celebrating? You are travelling alone, yes?" Captain Rasheed seemed confused.

"Yes, that is exactly the reason. I got divorced last month, and this cruise is my way of celebrating the return of my freedom." Robert embellished the truth a little, holding no great desire to tell his life story to the man, but he wanted to make sure they thought him to be a normal guy, not some crazy killer or super-secret black ops individual.

"Very good. You are free to leave, but, my friend, please do not tell anybody else about this man. It is disrespectful to talk of the dead, and people are here much like you. To have fun." Captain Rasheed rose from the table and offered his hand to Robert.

"Oh, I have no plans to say anything to anybody, you can trust me on that," Robert answered.

Captain Rasheed escorted him back to the main passenger elevator, saying nothing as they walked, but while they waited for the elevator to arrive, the captain moved in front of Robert and placed a hand on his shoulder. "If you feel sick, or unwell, please visit the doctor immediately, ok, my friend?"

Robert rode the lift alone, enjoying the silence, but he could not take his eyes from the corner spot. He could almost see the man's form, hunched over, his life slipping away from him. It did not matter that everything had happened in a different lift; the lingering spirit of the dead seemed to follow him.

Turning, Robert looked at his reflection in the mirror that formed the rear wall of the elevator. He looked pale. He realized that he was still covered in vomit. It had dried to a crust on his hands, and flaked away like an old scab. He needed a shower and a nap. Once he woke, then it would be time to reset everything, and get back to enjoying his trip.

CHAPTER 7

Jose and Sofia left their cabin and walked arm-in-arm, their bodies pressed close to one another. They headed to the lower levels first, deciding to start their journey from the ground up. They took their time, browsing through the food court and the bars. With the boat now full and ready to sail, plenty of passengers seemed to be on a similar journey of discovery. All eyes surveying the ship down to the smallest detail. Nobody paid anybody else any mind; the majesty of the ship consumed their attention, leaving no time to notice other passengers.

The only time the couple found their attention drawn away from the spectacle of the ship came when a young child ran into the bathroom, vomiting just before they reached the door. A frantic mother followed close behind, scooping the kid into her arms before bursting into the bathroom like a DEA agent at the start of a raid.

"That kid did not look very good," Sofia said, turning towards Jose.

"I'm sure they will be fine," Jose answered. He did not feel like standing around to find out, and so led his new bride away further into the ship.

The fourth deck served as the main entry point for passengers, and was the lowest level open to the public. It was home to the excursions help desk, which seemed to be staffed exclusively by attractive ladies barely out of their teens. All smiles and pretty faces. Always the perfect solution, whether it is for sales or complaints. A large storage locker area stood behind the lobby, a place for people to store their belongings should they so wish. Deck four also housed the first of the ships three cinemas and the lower level of the theatre, which spanned two decks, all told. There was also a simple self-service style café, which sold assorted light snacks. The ideal place for excursion days, giving people the chance to have a coffee and a croissant while they waited for the day to begin. A small cluster of fruit machines also stood in a small alcove by the reception desk, their flashing lights and muted sounds a sirens song to those desperate to part with some cash in their final minutes.

The couple walked around the deck, taking in the sights and sounds of the boat. They took the stairs up to deck five. On the main, grand staircase, each floor was broken into two short flights of stairs that met via a small landing. Halfway up to deck five, they came across a man sitting on the lower step of the second flight. His arms were wrapped around his body as if he was cold. He sat with his head resting on his knees. There was an odour of illness about him. Both smelled it as they walked by.

"We should check if he needs help," Sofia said, looking back at the man on the steps.

"I'm sure...look, there comes somebody now." Jose pointed to the two approaching figures. One was a security guard and the other, well, given how all uniforms seemed to be the same, the other person could have been anybody.

The pair walked up to the man and started talking to him.

"See, he is in good hands," Jose spoke, giving Sofia's hand a gentle squeeze.

"I hope he is alright." Sofia turned and walked with Jose into the main area of the deck.

"That is just one of the reasons why I love you so hard," Jose said, planting a kiss on the side of his wife's neck.

Sofia giggled, and sighed gently as one kiss became two, then three. She pushed Jose away with another giggle. "Let's take a look around. I am starving."

The hustle and bustle of the fifth deck helped clear their minds of the sick man. It seemed to be the main shopping deck, with the centre-most square of deck being a commercial arcade with shops selling everything from souvenirs and children's toys, to books, DVDs and even some high-end fashion stores.

As they moved around the shopping centre, they could be forgiven for forgetting that they were on a boat. It had the feel of a shopping mall or a city centre.

A cry went up behind them, drawing their attention away from the bookstore window. All of the most recent releases lined the window. Looking back the way they had come, a small crowd had gathered around the central lift. A highly polished bronze with glass walls, it only operated between decks four and five, but certainly added to the overall look of the ship.

"What's going on?" Sofia asked Jose.

"I don't know. Looks like somebody is lying on the floor. They fell or something." He strained his neck to look without making it too obvious. He did not want to become one of those people, the kind that gathered around straining to get a look at somebody else's misfortune.

"I hope that doesn't mean anything. First that guy and now this. The ship is making its maiden voyage. That has to be a bad omen or something." Sofia tightened her grip on Jose's hand.

"Come on, let's get something to eat." Jose felt the increased pressure of his wife's grip and knew they needed to leave.

The rear of the deck was reserved for cabins, while the front portion of the deck held both a small cinema which seemed to be lined up to play nothing but a string of romantic comedies, the lower level of the theatre, and also the main business area. Four large conference rooms led through to the promenade deck and a family restaurant.

The jungle-themed restaurant was not exactly the sort of restaurant either had in mind, but hunger insisted they pay it a visit. They walked in and took a seat. Half of the restaurant represented a full on jungle, plants and flowers lining the walls and ceiling. Display cases were built into one wall, which featured frogs, snakes and other jungle-based critters inside. The second half of the restaurant space catered for those that liked the theme, but wanted to avoid the realism. Jungle-themed paintwork and tables tops made to look like tree trunks would suffice for anybody that chose to sit there.

"Welcome to the Jungle, we promise fun and games. Welcome to the jungle, can I take your order?" A young and overly enthusiastic employee appeared by their table.

Jose looked at him with a smile. He gave it until the end of the first shift before that opening line got tiresome and forced.

"Thanks, can we get two cokes and a few minutes to study the menu?" Jose answered, looking at Sofia for confirmation on the order.

"Sure thing, sir, I'll be right back," the young Indian man answered with a broad and beaming smile.

The pair studied the menu together, laughing at the names given to the dishes. Their server, whose name badge christened him as being Alok, returned with their drinks.

The couple both ordered a burger and fries, with a side of coleslaw and onion rings to share. Alok smiled and turned to walk away. He gave a thick, rumbling cough as he did, his step hurried as he moved away from the table.

Sofia looked at Jose, her eyes wide with worry. He placed his hand on top of hers and gave it a gentle squeeze.

"What do you say that after this we can go back to the room, get changed and hit the pool area?" he said, offering a distraction.

"That sounds like fun." Sofia smiled.

Their food arrived, brought over by a different waiter. The portions were enormous and the quality superb. They cleared their plates and were left feeling full and happy. As they walked away, Sofia looked around for Alok, but could not find him.

A pit of worry had formed in her stomach. She could feel it there, twisting and turning, growing steadily larger and stronger. She did not know what caused it, but she did know it would not be going away anytime soon.

CHAPTER 8

Celia Darrow tossed and turned in her bed. Sleep claimed her almost the moment Derrick tucked her in. The fever hit a few minutes later, and she had been restless ever since. Moaning and groaning as she twisted and turned, trying to find a comfortable position. She woke twice, sitting bolt upright in bed, yanking the covers from her. Her eyes were wide and distant. The second time her eyes had a glazed-over look that gave her face a ghoulish expression.

Derrick tucked her back in each time, kissing her on her forehead, his worry increasing as fast as her fever seemed to be.

They decided that Carol should take their son Michael for a walk around the ship. He was a delicate child and the issues between husband and wife had affected him, even though they made sure to keep their squabbles away from the children. Seeing his sister sick always upset Michael, and so Carol offered to take him for some food and a play.

Derrick did not mind. He liked the quiet, and while he was trying his hardest, he still could not bring himself to fully move on from what had happened. He only agreed to try and salvage things because of the children.

He sat in one of the large armchairs, a bourbon and coke in the glass on the table. He sipped it gently, watching his daughter sleep, feeling just as restless as her.

The door to the room opened and Carol appeared, and a short way behind her came Michael, licking a large ice cream cone. Carol said nothing, but moved straight into the bathroom. The door slammed shut behind her and a few moments later the guttural sound of projectile vomiting came from behind the door. Michael stood in the doorway and stared at the bathroom door.

"Come on over here, sit down, you don't want to drip that all over the floor." Derrick rose to let his son sit down.

"Honey, honey, are you alright?" Derrick stood by the bathroom door.

"I'm fine," Carol snapped, snatching at her words between bouts of vomiting. With the door to the bathroom ajar, the stench of soured stomach contents wafted through into the cabin.

Derrick wrinkled his nose and pulled the door shut.

He moved back across the room and sat down beside Michael, who sat with the remote in hand, flicking through the channels moving from one to the other without so much as recognizing the show.

Derrick picked up his drink and took a long sip. Carol continued to vomit in the toilet, and in the bed beside him, Celia began to cry.

"Dad, is Mum alright?" Michael asked. "I don't like it here. Everybody is sick." Michael looked to be on the verge of tears. His ice cream was as good as untouched, something unheard of for Michael.

"No, no, of course not. Your mother just ate something funny, and your sister is just tired," Derrick lied. "She will be fine when she wakes up, and then we can take a look around the boat as a family. I heard that they have an aquarium on board. We can go check it out."

Michael sank back into the chair. "What about all of the others?" He looked at his father with hauntingly sunken eyes.

"What do you mean?" Derrick felt a chill run through him.

"Out there, everybody is sick. I saw them." Michael's face paled and his ice cream fell from his hands.

"He's right," Carol spoke. She emerged from the bathroom, her face beyond pale and her shirt sodden with sweat. She stumbled to the bed, barely able to support her own weight. She half collapsed onto the mattress and crawled up toward the pillows.

Derrick swallowed hard, a lump lodged in his throat.

"I'm sure it just looked that way." He didn't know what to say.

"No, there is something wrong. People are sick. Real sick." Carol spoke, her voice coming in a whisper.

On the other bed, Celia had fallen still, her cries silenced, replaced by a rapid breathing that sounded more like panting, as if she has just finished a race. Derrick looked from his wife to his daughter and back again.

Reaching out, he picked up the phone to call reception. He knew there was a medical bay on the ship; he just hoped the doctor would make a visit to the room.

The voice that answered the phone on the eleventh ring did not have the friendly tone that welcomed them aboard. The young voice sounded stressed and rushed.

"Hello, this is Mr. Darrow in room 7132. I just wanted to ask if there is a doctor on board who could maybe pay a visit to the room?" Derrick asked as he tried to calm his mind down. The situation in the room continued to worsen, the general odour of sickness was everywhere, and his wife seemed to be following a similar path to his daughter. Carol's slide into the illness seemed to be happening faster than Celia.

On the chair behind him, Derrick heard his son begin to sob.

"It's all going to be alright, Michael. I promise." Derrick covered the mouthpiece of the phone with his hand, while on the other end of the line the receptionist was busy explaining that due to a current rush of appointments, the medical bay could not accommodate any more appointments. She finished by saying anybody showing signs of a flu-like illness should stay in bed and drink plenty of water.

The line disconnected as soon as the woman finished talking, leaving Derrick no opportunity to reply. Derrick felt a flash of anger rise up in him. He picked up the receiver again and tried to call back down to ask to speak to the duty manager. The line was busy, which only added to the uneasy feeling growing in Derrick's stomach.

Derrick checked on the patients, both seeming to have fallen into a deep sleep. Their hearts raced and sweat slicked their skin, but their temperatures seemed to have come down. Celia's forehead felt cooler to his touch, and the fire-red flush no longer glowed in her cheeks.

"Hey, Mike, I need to pop outside for a few minutes. Do you want to come with me?" Derrick asked.

Michael looked at his dad, then at his mother and sister, and finally back to his dad. "Do you have to go?" The fear in his voice was absolute.

"I'll only be a few minutes. I just need to check on something and see if I can buy some medicine," Michael answered him.

"I'll stay here. I don't want to go out there. People are sick." Michael pulled his feet up onto the seat of the chair, and rested his chin on his knees, disappearing into the safe world of cartoons.

An overly sensitive child, Michael always seemed to pick up on things before anybody else. It bordered on being spooky at times, some form of pre-cognition. Derrick knew that there would be no changing his son's mind, and so turned to leave, grabbing the spare key from the desk as he went.

The empty hallway seemed full of ominous portent, but Derrick told himself that everybody had either found their rooms or already inserted themselves into various venues around the ship. Still, he walked with cautious steps, the sway of the boat was great or rather, more perceptible in the corridor.

Taking the lift down to deck four, Derrick thought through what he was going to say. He understood that it was the first trip for the boat, and most likely the first time that some of the staff members were going to be faced with so many passengers and calls. He did not want to cause trouble, but with two sick family members in the room, the attitude he received over the phone rubbed him up the wrong way.

The lift stopped at every deck on the way down, with a seemingly endless chain of people getting on and off. Derrick found himself crammed into the back, pressed against the mirror. This gave Derrick ample opportunity to draw in the odour of his fellow passengers. The mix of sweaty, raw, naked human flesh and a range of deodorants and colognes was a heady one. It left Derrick feeling quite unwell by the time the doors opened. He understood how passengers could get sick being stuck in such confined conditions. The rest, he knew from experience, would take care of itself. A queasy feeling from being crammed into a tightly populated place could easily manifest itself with headaches and nausea. Add a hot flush and a need to lie down, and suddenly you have the flu.

By the time he reached the reception desk, Derrick's rage had all but vanished. Given his wife's history of travel sickness and the fact that a young child was more likely to get sick than a fully-grown adult, Derrick realized the depth of his overreaction. He was tired, and their holiday seemed to be starting on a sour note. That did not give him the right to take his frustrations out on the young crewmembers.

The reception desk was busy, with three young girls standing behind it, the front line for the continual stream of questions. Even at a first glance, Derrick saw three people with white-knuckled fists resting on the counter, a couple of women crying and a handful of people standing around demonstrating wildly with their arms. Derrick stopped, turned around and headed back to his room. He felt sorry for them.

Derrick paused short of joining their numbers. The young women behind the counter looked as if they were about to drop, with tired, strained expressions and a generally exhausted appearance. By the time the lift doors closed, Derrick realized he would not change places with those young women for all the tea in China.

The lift was full, meaning that each time it stopped, the rush of departing bodies forced Derrick out of the lift and onto the deck. The rush of people eager to squeeze into the rising elevator on deck six caused him to miss his ride. Knowing how long it would take before another arrived, he decided to use the stairs, but not before having a quick look around. He had been sitting in the cabin for hours. He needed some fresh air and to clear his head from the lift induced giddiness.

He walked down the corridor, heading toward the front of the ship, not really paying attention to those around him. He did see a formidable-looking queue forming for the cinema, which promised a showing of the latest Pixar release. The large children's play area situated opposite a fast food court and general lounging area also seemed to be quite the popular place, judging from the hoots and hollers that came from inside.

As he moved along the ship, taking it in for the first time since arriving, having been busy herding the children the first time, Derrick was blown away by not only the size but the services on board. He had skimmed the brochure, but not really absorbed everything about the layout and the facilities that the ship offered. The observation deck was busy but not crowded. Groups of people stood leaning against the railings watching the Dubai skyline pass them by, photos and tablets raised to the sky. So many people lost in capturing the moment time and time again that they completely missed the opportunity to live in it, to enjoy it.

While the temperature outside was high, the motion of the boat created a gentle wind that cleared Derrick's head. He stood against the railings and allowed his mind to wander. Wander away from the potentially sick family, and away from his cheating wife, who, in spite of her best efforts, broke his heart all over again every time she looked at him. Derrick allowed his mind to wander away into nothing, into the world of daydreams and fantasy.

Moving back inside, Derrick made his way to their room. He did not realize how late it was. His stomach growled, and he thought a nice dinner for anybody who could manage it would be a great way to get things back on track.

Carol and Celia were still deep in sleep, their breathing fast and erratic, but their bodies seemed more relaxed, and their faces no longer held the strained look of troubled slumber. Michael still sat in the same spot. He was wearing clean clothes and the ice cream stains had been washed from his hands and face. His dirty clothes lay in a heap over the floor. He was colouring, while in the background, a football match had broken out on the television. It had taken a long time before Michael had shown a real interest in anything, and then came football. Michael watched one game, and that was it. His life seemed to revolve around the sport. He followed two different teams in two leagues and knew their players, the scores of every game.

"Hey, champ, it looks like those two are out for the night. Why don't we let them get some rest and head down for some food?" Derrick offered." I saw some pretty cool stuff just now, too, so maybe we can hit the bowling alley or the arcade."

"I want to have a swim." Michael looked over at his dad. His eyes were swollen from tears, his face pale and pasty.

"Sure, we can take a look at the pools." Michael jumped up from the table, a smile on his face, while Derrick grabbed their swimming gear and checked on the patients.

"I'll be back soon. Get some rest," he whispered to Celia, who stirred a little as he kissed her forehead.

The restaurant looked busy, so they decided to just grab a hamburger and a milkshake from the fifth deck and then head out for a swim.

The pools were located on the Lido deck, or rather, deck twelve. It was clear that this was one of the main decks because the minute they stepped outside, the mass of people around them seemed to grow exponentially. Sun loungers littered the deck, filled with bodies every shade of red, orange and peach that could be named. Young muscled bodies and bikini-clad women strolled arm-in-arm around the deck, or lay atop one another on the loungers. Kids ran and screamed, splashing in any one of the three pools. The two bars also had a line of people ready to get their drink on. Derrick soon added himself to the list, while Michael disappeared into the pool. While a technically strong swimmer, more than capable to be left to his own devices, Derrick wanted to sit close by just in case. He found a seat close by the water, and deposited their belongings on it.

Derrick sat with his drink, enjoying the sun on his skin, watching his son play in the water. He had even made a friend, or so it would seem. Friends were something Michael found difficult to make. He was often too shy to join in the boisterousness of boys' play, and too afraid of being pointed out if he did anything too feminine. Derrick had spent many hours talking to his son, telling him that it didn't matter what he did, as long as he was happy doing it.

It was noisy on the deck, but not disturbing. A constant source of sound, from screams and shouts of pleasure, to the odd cry of pain, as children did what children do, and came running in all directions with stubbed toes, scraped knees and thick lips.

The sun began to lower on the horizon and the deck slowly started to clear. People began heading off for late dinners, evening shows and entertainment, or at least to start the necessary preparations for later in the night.

By the time they got back to the room, Michael could barely keep his eyes open, and leaned heavily on his dad.

"That was fun. Can we do it again tomorrow? I loved the pool, and my friend Jack said he will be there, too." Michael smiled, beaming ear-to-ear.

"Sure thing, buddy. This is your holiday, too. I just hope that tomorrow your mum and sister can join us." Derrick opened the door and slid into the room. The odour of illness was still strong, but they found Carol sitting up in bed looking much brighter.

Celia still slept.

"She hasn't moved," Carol said, her voice a whisper. Even in the dim light of the room, Derrick could see the colour on his wife's cheeks.

"You feeling better?" he asked

"Much. I think it was just the travel and the long day. I'm tired, though. I think I'm going to have an early night," Carol answered.

"That sounds like a grand idea," Derrick said as he took the remote control and dropped onto the bed beside his wife.

The rest of his family were asleep when Derrick heard the first scream. Lying in bed, he could not make himself fall asleep. Even with the television turned off and the room plunged into total darkness, his brain would not shut down.

Another scream came, ripping through night's shroud. A few moments later, something crashed against the door. What sounded like a scuffle followed next, with thumping footsteps moving at a run coming soon after.

Derrick got out of bed and stood in the darkness. The others did not stir. They slept on, oblivious. He strained his ears to listen. More screams rang out in the distance. Derrick shuddered at their blood-curdling pitch.

They were not shrieks of pleasure, nor were they cries of surprise. They were unlike anything Derrick had heard before and their lingering echo terrified him down to his boots.

The corona of light that framed the door in the darkness flickered, disappearing for a long count of three before coming back on.

A few moments later, all hell broke loose.

CHAPTER 9

Eric Brown wandered around the ship without a care in the world. His smile spread ear-to-ear, and for the first time in a great many years, everything felt good. *God is good,* Eric thought to himself. He smiled, having just finished a wonderful dinner in the BBQ Grill house located on deck seven. The flavours used on the meat had set his mouth ablaze. Even now, as stuffed as he felt, the idea of the food made his mouth water.

The deck boasted two different lounges and a bar. The latter caught Eric's attention. The grand opening of the casino on the lower decks seemed to have drawn most people to it like ants to a picnic. Not much of a gambler, besides the odd bet on a football game every now and then, Eric felt no strong desire to head down and throw away his money. Although, he planned on visiting it once in the coming days, just to see what all the fuss was about.

Settling into the bar, he ordered a beer and sat back.

Sitting by the tall panoramic windows, Eric looked out at the ocean. With the sun disappearing from view, a darkness fell and offered a form of night far different from what Eric was used to. So far out at sea, away from the rest of the world and the lights and structures of life, the concept of night held a new meaning. It was relaxing, a darkness that brought with it no fear or monsters lurking within the shadows. It was soothing and calm.

Time moved on, and Eric sat at peace. He sipped his drink and looked at the stars. He had long been fascinated by them and the possibilities they held. What was up there? The potential for good and evil, just waiting in space for man to come along and put it to use. Would humanity be the first or the last to find it, would they find a way to turn it against one another? Eric's mind once again became a constant stream of thoughts and questions, notions and ponderings. At times, he cursed his artist's brain. He could never just shut off and drift away on a thought. Not without a hundred questions and different ideas being thrown back at him.

Eric had struggled with his thoughts and that side of himself for a long time. It took several years before he found a peace with himself, and his less-than-everyday view of the world. It had been a struggle through adolescence and high school, but now, as an adult, he balked at the idea of being any other way.

"Hey there, fancy seeing you here," a friendly voice rang out, breaking his train of thought.

Eric tumbled from being among the stars, back to the bar, back to the boat. He turned his head and saw Tara looking at him, wearing an elegant black dress, which hugged her figure and made her look even more attractive for it.

"It's a small world," Eric said, hoping the heat on his cheeks came from the sun and beer.

"Mind if I join you?" she asked, pointing to the chair on the other side of the table.

"Sure, I'd like that very much," Eric answered, looking around as he sat up straighter in the chair. The bar was still far from full; there were plenty of empty tables. That meant Tara chose to sit with him. That made him slightly nervous.

The pair got talking, and before long sat comfortably with one another, chatting about their life and what made them decide to take a cruise. They spoke like friends, age-old acquaintances, catching up on lost years.

The drink they shared turned into multiple of the same, and before the night was out they moved away from the chairs and over to a sofa-style seat in the corner or the lounge. Sitting side-by-side, they laughed and flirted with one another. Oblivious to the rest of the world.

The bar grew busier, which rather ironically afforded them even more privacy, because the eager eyes that found them so easily before, now needed to search that much harder, and found themselves presented with a wider range of far more interesting options.

Eric woke with a start. Normally he was one to rise to the surface of wakefulness only with the aid of a large cup of coffee.

Yet now, he was awake and alert in an instant. Something wrenched him from sleep, and while it pained him, he could not accredit it to the beautiful blonde woman who lay naked beside him. Tara slept deeply, her face relaxed and content.

Eric's head was a little fuzzy, but he could still remember every moment of their evening, both in the bar and back in his cabin. He remembered how they made good use of the mini bar, and the auto feed mechanism that powered it.

They also thoroughly tested the shower, coming out dirtier than when they went in.

Eric found his eyes lingering on the Tara, his eyes tracing the contours of her body beneath the blanket.

Getting out of the bed, Eric moved through the room to the bathroom. His bare feet squelched on the wet carpet by the bathroom door. Eric paused, his feet cold and wet. He did not realize that they had made that much of a mess together. He smiled to himself. Not once did he imagine he would ever share a bed with a woman like Tara.

Inside the bathroom, Eric turned on the light and looked around. The floor was dry, the only sign of their presence being the pile of clothes that lay strewn over the floor.

Turning, Eric looked back into the room's small hallway. The carpet was dark and wet. Eric looked down at his feet. They were covered in blood, and the scarlet outline of his footprints came in from the hall.

Eric's legs left him and he fell against the counter. His head spun as he tried to think back through the evening. Hoping to recall a moment where an injury occurred. A sudden and paralysing thought hit Eric like a truck. He ran from the bathroom, his feet slapping in the blood-soaked carpet. Reaching the bed, he turned on the light and pulled back the bed covers.

"What? What's happening?" Tara cried out, ripped from sleep.

"Blood...there is blood everywhere," Eric said, the words spilling from his mouth before he had the chance to realize how crazy it sounded.

"What? I don't...I think I should leave." Tara slid from the bed, holding the covers against her, hiding her body but not her fear.

She moved slowly toward the bathroom, walking backward, not taking her eyes off Eric. She disappeared into the room, not noticing the wet floor, although her scream a few moments later put that to rights.

Eric appeared in the bathroom doorway. Tara sat with her legs pulled up against her body on the sink counter, her knees drawn to her chest. Blood dripped from her feet, splashing on the white-tiled floor.

"What did...that's blood...where..." She spat the words, her eyes running frantically around the room, her breaths coming faster and faster until she verged on hyperventilation.

"I don't know. I thought you were hurt, that's why I woke you...oh god, it's coming from under the door." Eric turned on the main bedroom lights and saw the thick layer of crimson fluid that sat atop the carpet.

"Is it really blood?" Tara asked, her mind still reeling and half asleep.

"Yes, it's blood. You can smell it." Eric turned to look at her. "I'm going to open the door and take a look."

Tara jumped off the counter and into his arms in an instant. "No!" she begged him. "You can't go out there. It's dangerous."

Eric managed to loosen himself from her grip. "It's ok. I'm just going to open the door and take a look around. I won't go anywhere." While he spoke calmly, panic bounced around inside him. So much so that he failed to realize that the beautiful naked woman standing in his bathroom was actually worried about his safety.

Tara left the bathroom and moved quickly to the bed, jumping over the bloody pool by the bathroom door. Watching from a safe distance, she gasped as Eric grabbed the handle, turned the lock and opened the door. The door opened inwards, and the weight pressing down against the door from the other side did all the work for him, once Eric opened the latch. The headless body fell back into the room, landing with a wet splat.

Eric jumped back and cried out in surprise. Behind him, Tara screamed.

"Close the door, close the door," she repeated over and over.

Eric listened to her advice. He pushed the body with his feet, sliding it out of the room and back into the hallway. He closed the door and locked it, all the time feeling vomit rising in his throat.

Turning to Tara, Eric jumped forward and scooped her into his arms as she fainted. Catching her, Eric held her against him, and placed her on the bed. The two of them were still as naked as the day they were born.

Once he finished vomiting in the bathroom, Eric made getting dressed the next order of business.

Tara came too, as Eric finished pulling his t-shirt over his head. "Do you have something for me? I don't want to go back over there." She spoke, sounding calmer and more lucid than at any point since their trip took a turn toward a bad horror movie.

"I don't know if you will like it," Eric began.

"Trust me, if it covers me up, I'll love it." Tara said pulling herself into a sitting position. "Everything seemed to be going so well, too."

"What do you mean?" Eric asked without thinking.

"Well, all of this. It was nice, and I certainly had fun." She looked at Eric, her eyes focused on his. "Or did you not have fun?"

"Oh…yeah, I thought so, too. I…." Eric searched for the right words.

"Easy, tiger. I'm just playing. A bad time for jokes I guess, but it's my way when I am stressed."

"I like it." Eric said, finding his thoughts. He handed Tara a t-shirt and a pair of shorts. The shorts were a little big in the waist, but the shirt looked much better on her, especially with her braless chest, than it ever did on him.

Dressed, they sat together on the bed. Hands together, they waited for what they knew would come. The screaming started, and not long after, a voice came over the loudspeaker.

CHAPTER 10

After being released from his interrogation at the hands of Captain Rasheed, a man who reminded him more and more of Inspector Clouseau than he did Poirot, or any of the other great fictional detective, Robert returned to his room.

Once there, he showered, changed and grabbed a soda from the mini bar. He was thirsty, almost insatiably so. He also hoped the sugar from the drinks would give him the energy burst that he needed in order to carry on. His interaction with the dead man left a lingering mark that Robert knew would take some time to fade away.

Feeling better, his head clear and his body more under his own control, and less likely to collapse under his own weight, Robert went back out to explore the ship.

A long-time runner, Robert headed up to the eleventh deck, which the ever-helpful TV map told him was the ship's sports centre.

The deck appeared to be a quiet area of the ship, although the batting cages that occupied a central section of the deck held a certain draw with the younger crowd. Robert spotted a juice bar and a restaurant that served health by the plate. The gym lay to his right at the far end of the deck, and from the outside looked to be larger than most sporting establishments Robert had ever been in. The running track ran along the edge of the deck, like a moat, protecting the rest of the sports equipment from invasion.

While not really in the mood to go for a run, Robert found the fresh air of the running track emptied his head and blew away the heavy thoughts that still clung on to his consciousness. He moved at a gentle jog, not looking to exert himself too much. He would have been a liar, however, if he said that the thud of his feet and the rhythm his brain created from them was not a hypnotic and therapeutic experience.

The sun sank low into the horizon, and the ocean danced a myriad of colours as it reflected the sky, as well as providing its own reflected smorgasbord of beauty.

Stopping after his fourth lap, Robert stood on the track and looked out to sea. The only one on the track, Robert took the chance to enjoy both the view and the solitude.

"Help me, somebody, please." The cry shattered the peace, causing Robert to jump. Spinning around, his heart racing, he saw people running in all directions, their screams a wall of noise. He saw a woman standing in the middle of it all. She could not have been much out of her teens, barely a woman at all in terms of age. She was covered in blood. It spurted from her throat in thin jets. She stumbled around, her hands clawing at her throat as if she could simply pull away the wound and discard it on the floor.

At first, Robert thought the swarm of running bodies were flocking to help her. The truth, he realized, revealed different motivations. People ran from the woman, ignoring her injuries and pleas for help. Robert sprinted around the track, leaving via the first offered exit. He pushed his way through the crowd, who seemed to be running in a blind panic, rather than with any real sense of purpose or direction. He reached the woman as she collapsed, and for the second time that day, Robert Nash found himself holding onto a corpse. Lowering her to the floor, Robert saw the extent of the wound in her throat.

From his earlier position on the running track, Robert assumed the injury to have been some sort of accident, either from the batting cages or with one of the machines in the gym. As he closed the distance to the woman, and saw the blood pouring from her wounds, he knew something more serious had happened. Robert dropped to the floor beside the girl. Blood spurted into his face from the vicious-looking gash in her flesh.

Robert looked at the wound; the curved, ridged edges somehow looked familiar. It was a bite mark, there could be no denying it. Somebody on the ship had bitten the woman's throat out.

"Don't leave me," she groaned as Robert adjusted his position.

"I won't. Help is coming. Here, put pressure on it," Robert said, removing his shirt to hold it against the woman's throat.

"I'm scared," she gasped.

She died before Robert found the time or the words to say anything comforting in her final moments.

Robert began to tremble. In less than twenty-four hours on the ship, two people had died, and he was present for both of them. He knew that in all likelihood Captain Rasheed would be looking for him, and that his questions would be more serious the second time around.

All around him, people continued to run. They paid no attention to Robert, or the blood-covered, half-eaten woman on the floor.

Looking around, Robert realized why everybody abandoned the woman when she needed them. The people that had attacked her were still close by, and they were not yet finished.

Farther down the deck, in the direction of the gym, he saw an ambling figure. It walked with a slow, shuffling gait, like that of a drunken man at the end of a long walk home. He was covered in blood, but unlike the woman, it did not flow from his wounds, but rather, it coated him.

The deck cleared and suddenly, Robert found himself alone. Just him, the dead woman and the shambling figure, which had drawn close enough for Robert to hear the feral growl that came from his throat. Beneath the bloody mask, the man's face was pale and his eyes clouded over white, as if stricken with cataracts.

Robert shuffled backwards, pulling himself along the floor, trying to rise as he went without turning his back on the thing that ambled his way.

Once on his feet, Robert turned and ran. The thing showed no sign of urgency; its pace remained slow and steady.

It reached the body and stopped. It raised its head and looked around before dropping to the deck. The creature lowered its head toward the corpse and, without hesitation, bit down into the still warm flesh. Wrenching its neck like a wild beast in the Serengeti, the man ripped away a thick chunk of juicy meat from the woman's cheek and swallowed it down before returning for another helping.

Robert felt his stomach turn against him. He bent over and vomited over the deck, a loud and choking expulsion that caught the attention of the cannibal. His face snapped around and he glared at Robert. Turning, Robert ran from the open-air portion of the deck. The doors were closed, and a sea of faces stared back at him.

"Let me in," Robert roared, pounding on the glass.

The faces stared at him, but made no move to open the door, especially when the figure appeared behind him. Their screams from inside the boat were clear. Robert turned away, already knowing what he would see.

The creature, for it could no longer still be considered a man, stood on the curve of the deck, blocking any route of escape that Robert may have entertained. In its hand, the creature held the severed arm of the woman. Long tendrils of torn flesh and stringy tendons dangled from the shoulder end of the limb.

Robert heard the panic erupt behind him, screams and shouts. Something else was inside. Faced with no other choice, Robert knew he needed to back around the deck toward the gym. The second set of doors there would allow him back into the inner portion of the ship. That just meant moving around the creature.

Robert waited. The thing made no attempt to run, content to shamble ever closer, its mouth still chewing on a wad of raw meat. It seemed to have no interest in further consuming the arm it carried.

Robert knew he could outrun the thing. All he needed to do was avoid being caught. Behind him, something crashed against the glass. He turned to see it smeared with blood, the contents of some poor fool's skull leaking down the door in thick grey globs.

Running, Robert charged as fast as his legs would move. He got beyond the creature and around the corner before the thing even reacted. His flight stopped momentarily when he came face-to-face with the young woman. Her body had been torn apart. Her flayed flesh and discarded organs littered the deck. Her chest had been ripped open, the ribcage torn apart and flung in all directions. Her head was a mass of raw meat, and the gaping hole where her shoulder socket should have connected with an arm made Robert want to vomit again.

Behind him, the creature growled, and shattered the freezing fear that held him. The doors at the other end of the deck looked to be clear. Robert charged through them and collapsed to the floor. He was tired, his breaths coming deep and sharp. However hard he tried, he seemed unable to take in enough oxygen to meet the demands of his panicked body. Yet he refused to stop. All around him screams resonated. Panicked and disoriented, Robert found the stairwell and started down it.

He hadn't gotten far before a siren began to sound, a high-pitched whistle that blasted continually. It sounded far too high-pitched to belong to such a large and manly vessel, but the voice that followed the blasts put to rest any doubts people may have held.

CHAPTER 11

"Captain, we've got reports of some sort of problem on the lower decks." Jeff Wilcox relayed the message as it came to him.

"What sort of problem, Mr. Wilcox?" Captain Sheen replied.

"Fuck if I know, it sounded as if all hell had broken loose. To be honest, it sounded like a fucking war zone. I heard people crying and screaming," Jeff replied.

Captain Sheen gave a sigh. "I really hoped this would be an uneventful trip. It is probably a group of yobs getting pissed in the sun causing a bit of a ruckus. Send security to sort it out." Sheen gave the order without worry.

The bridge was quiet. During the night, the bridge operated on a skeleton crew. Sheen himself was preparing to retire to his Captain's cabin for a few hours of rest. The crew accommodations on deck fourteen offered a more luxurious set-up than the other cruise ships either Jeff or Joe had worked on.

"Captain, I'm not getting any response from the security office," Jeff called out, looking across at his old friend.

Sheen paused for a second. A look flashed in his XO's eyes. One he had not seen very many times before. "How do you mean?"

"I mean there is nothing there. The line is dead." Jeff swallowed hard as he spoke. "Want me to go down and take a look myself?"

"No, let's not go crazy. I need you here on the bridge. Ibrahim, can you go check out the problems. Head down to deck four and see what's going on," the captain spoke to one of the night watch, and smiled as the man hurried away as if Sheen were some great military general.

"I've got a bad fucking feeling about this," Jeff whispered as he moved beside Sheen.

"Relax. You are just worked up because of the threat they intercepted before we left." Sheen placed a hand on his XO's shoulder. "I tell you what, why don't you take the first rest. I'll stay on shift and come get you at oh-three-hundred."

"It's not the threat. It's…you didn't hear them. I've heard drunks causing problems before. Fucking shit, you must remember what happened in the Maldives when that guy went postal after catching his wife banging a couple of dudes from the bar. I'm telling you, this is different. I heard screaming, people in pain, man. Plus…well, I'm not sure how to say it…it was like a growl." Jeff shook his head, unable to find the right words to express what he had heard.

"Ok, well, let's say this is something serious. We are locked away up here and we have constant contact with at least two different ports at all times during the trip. We are safe as houses up here. This thing is state of the art." Sheen stood and moved behind the central console.

He looked out at the water, the millpond surface. The stars littered the cloudless sky. It was Joe's favourite time of day to be out on the ocean. The stars fascinated him, and out on the open ocean, so far away from everything, he found the sense of freedom that eluded him so successfully when he was on land.

"I guess you're right. Listen to me, prattling on like a fucking rookie missing his mum." Jeff laughed his concerns away, and while it may have sounded convincing to the crew, he knew he did not believe it himself. The look he got from Joe said that he had not fooled the captain, either.

With the ship's course set for the night and their speed reduced to not much more than a drift, they had plenty of time to play with before they needed to make their first stop.

Jeff paced nervously around the bridge, an act that slowly started to spread to the others. The atmosphere changed. Joe could feel it happening. He looked at his friend, and could not recall ever seeing Joe so worked up.

"How about we head back to my cabin and have a cup of tea. I could certainly use one," he spoke after a time.

"Um, yeah, actually, I could do with a drink." Jeff nodded, turning to look at the remaining crew.

They looked on edge. Ibrahim had yet to return after more than an hour. To top it off, the phone lines were not being answered, at either reception, the sick bay or even on the security deck.

"Omar, you have the bridge until I return. Hold the course steady, speed is constant. There shouldn't be anything to worry about." No sooner had Joe spoke, and something crashed against the bridge's main door.

The bridge had been designed with maximum security protocols. There had been an unconfirmed threat received earlier that morning, which resulted in the decision being made to operate on full lockdown. It meant that nobody other than the captain or his XO could access the bridge from the outside. Everybody else needed to go through video display clearance.

"Ahmad, check the video feed. I want to see who it is," Captain Sheen barked, surprised at how on edge he was.

The man didn't speak but gave a salute, as the whole crew seemed to do when either the captain or the XO addressed them. The young crewmember checked the video screens and gave a cry in his native language.

Neither Jeff nor Joe understood what he said, but within moments, the remaining crew were running toward the door, a clamour of shouts and calls echoing around the bridge.

"What is it?" Joe asked rising to his feet.

"What's going on?" Jeff followed suit.

Before either man knew it, the door to the bridge opened and the agitated crewmembers rushed outside.

They returned quickly, carrying a blood-covered body with them. The door closed quickly behind them. In a murmured panic, the group laid the body down on the floor.

"It's Ibrahim," Jeff said, startled. He turned to look at his captain. "What the fuck is going on out there?"

"I have no idea. Zahi, I want you to sound the emergency alarm. I want people to the survival areas, consolidated into places where we can watch them. Issam, keep trying to get in touch with the security teams. We need to hear back from them." Joe gave the orders, his head calm in the emotional storm.

While Joe took control of the ship, Jeff moved to the injured man, who thrashed against those who tried to hold him down.

"What happened to him?" Jeff asked, crouching down beside the man. Deep lacerations covered head and scalp, leaving his face a battered and bloody mess. There was a second gaping wound on his torso, and a third on his leg.

"We need to control the bleeding. Get me the first aid kit and try to contact the medical ward. You two, help me get his shirt off. We need to hurry." Jeff was no stranger to working triage. During his years in the Navy, Jeff had been on the wrong side of a few different skirmishes. It had been a long time, but he found himself sliding back into his training with ease.

Together they managed to cut away Ibrahim's shirt, revealing the full extent of his injuries.

"These look like bite marks," Jeff said as he studied the wounds. Blood poured from them like a dark red flood. "I need towels and water. Some alcohol too, we need to clean the wounds. If these are bites, we don't want them getting infected."

Nobody moved. They all looked at Jeff with expressions of terror plastered on their faces.

"He is going to die unless you help me," he roared at them. "Joe, call for a chopper. We need to get him off the ship."

Joe understood the seriousness of the situation, and accepted that his XO was better suited to take charge, and dutifully obeyed the order he was given.

"Shit in a fucking basket, if nobody wants to go, I'll do it." Jeff stood up and glared at the crew. "Just hold him still, keep him cool, it feels like he is on fire. I'll be back."

"Jeff," Joe called.

"Don't worry. I've got everything we need in my room, I'll be a couple of minutes, tops," Jeff answered, knowing exactly what his friend was going to say.

"We don't know what's going on out there," Joe replied.

"No, but it did that," he said, pointing at the injured Ibrahim. "Patching him up comes first. Have you put the word out for the medi-helo?"

"Yes, they will be here in twenty," Joe answered.

"Good, this will all blow over. Just make sure the passengers are quarantined in the evac zones. We will clear the ship and have everything back under control by morning," Jeff lied. He could feel the ball of fear gestating in his gut.

"Be quick," Joe said. He had worked with Jeff long enough to know when there was no talking him out of his plan.

Jeff didn't say anything else, but keyed in the code to the door and was out into the hallway before he had the chance to think about it.

The bridge was on the uppermost deck. It consisted of a small corridor that gave access to a small kitchen area and the crew canteen. Between the two rooms, a single staircase led down to the crew quarters.

Once outside of the bridge, Jeff could hear the echoed screams of those in the lower levels. They bounced through the ship like the melancholy cry of ghosts in a mansion.

Jeff hurried down the stairs to the crew level. The XO and Captain's cabins sat closest to the stairwell, giving them the shortest distance to the bridge. They had the largest rooms on the deck, and while they were very nice for crew accommodation, they did not hold a candle to the passenger facilities.

Jeff expected the corridor to be quiet, empty even; he did not expect to find a severed arm lying on the floor in a pool of blood.

Jeff stopped in his tracks, but did not freeze. He knew that to freeze could mean his death. Forcing himself on, Jeff sprinted to his room, pulled open the door and disappeared inside. He stopped before closing the door, taking the chance to look up and down the hall. He wanted to know what he was up against. He saw nothing, but the hungry growls that rumbled his way could not have come from the lower decks.

Jeff gathered the things he needed, including towels, and a bottle of vodka, which he had acquired from the bar on the seventh floor. Jeff also grabbed the first-aid kit from his cabin's bathroom. Before he left, however, he paused. Pondering for just a couple of seconds, he turned away from the door and moved to his bed. He fumbled around and pulled out a lock box. Sliding the combination into place, he opened it and pulled out the revolver that sat there. He slid the slip into place and checked the safety before sliding the weapon into the back of his trousers.

He opened the door and looked out. The hall was empty, including the severed limb. Jeff immediately sought it out.

Something growled, and Jeff pulled himself back into his room. Knowing he had to move, Jeff opened the door once more and peered into the corridor. Nothing. He could still hear the echoing cries of the passengers, and the faint instructions being issued by the captain for everybody to report to the nearest emergency location.

Stepping into the corridor, Jeff found his legs growing sluggish. His years in the cruise industry had made him soft, especially around the middle. As he stepped away from the safety of his room, the scent of blood grew stronger.

Another growl, and a door closed with a sudden crash.

Jeff spun around and saw the two figures standing mid-way down the hallway. He could make out their gore-encrusted frames even from distance. It left no room for confusion with regard to their intentions.

"Stop, I am an officer of this ship. You need to stop this act right now. You hurt one of our crew," Jeff began, facing the pair. "We have help flying in. You will be detained and removed from this ship immediately."

The figures growled a response and stumbled forward. They moved with jagged steps, devoid of all of the rhythm and fluidity of normal motion.

"I don't know what you have taken, but I am ordering you to stop," Jeff called, taking a step away from the pair.

The figures continued, and as they drew closer, Jeff got a better look at them. One was missing an ear, while the left hand side of their face resembled a bubbling lump of minced meat. The other, a woman, had a hole in her gut. Something had stabbed through and caught, tearing a wide jagged wound that stretched from the curve of her belly up to just below her ribs.

Jeff pulled his gun. "Stay back."

They stared at him, their eyes a milky white. They growled, lips pulling back to reveal blood-stained teeth.

Jeff fired a round, hitting the man in the leg. He continued moving, an extra degree of limp added to his gait.

"What the hell are you on?" he asked them as he took a step closer to the stairs.

They showed no inclination to hurry, and their confidence seemed overwhelming. Jeff knew he could beat them up the stairs in a run. He had the head start, but if they did decide to give chase, he could not be sure if the door to the bridge would be opened in time to save him.

They advanced even closer, and the scent of death was heavy on their persons.

Jeff fired another shot, his adrenaline surging once more. The bullet penetrated the man's chest with a burst of skin and a trickle of blood. It knocked the man to the floor. An act seemingly unnoticed by his female companion, for she continued to advance, her growls growing hungrier by the second.

To Jeff's horror, the man on the floor began to thrash around, and after managing to haul himself to his feet, he too continued his advance.

"Holy shit," Jeff whispered, backing up quicker now.

He turned and bolted up the stairs, not too masculine to give in to the fact that the situation terrified him. He reached the bridge door and pounded on it, his fist slamming against the metal door, even as it opened. Jeff jumped inside and helped the crew push the door closed.

Panting and sweating, he said nothing for a moment, and the others let him be. They all saw the supplies clenched under his arm, and more importantly, the gun in his other hand.

"Jeff," Joe stood and stared at the gun.

"They...there are people down there, on the crew deck. They are...I don't fucking know, but I shot one of them, in the fucking chest and the damned thing just stood back up." Jeff slid the weapon back into the belt of his trousers, and handed the supplies to Zahi, who stood waiting to take them.

"What are you talking about?" the captain asked.

"Here, wet these, keep one on his head at all times. We need to clean the wounds, too. Use the vodka and wash him down," Jeff instructed before he moved toward Joe.

"I'm talking about the impossible, Joe. I'm saying those things down there, those people, they are covered in blood, and well...fuck...motherfuck...they are dead. As dead as anything could be. Yet fuck me, there they are walking around as if nothing was wrong at all." Jeff knew he sounded crazy, but he had seen them with his own eyes.

"Are you trying to tell me the dead have risen aboard this ship?" Joe asked, trying hard to keep his voice serious.

"Yes, that's what I'm telling you. We need more help. We need to get evacuated or something." Jeff held the captain's gaze until Joe began to nod.

"I believe you. It's fucked up and crazier than a badger playing the banjo, but I have known you long enough to know when you are telling the truth.

"Sir, he's dying," a voice called out.

Jeff turned and moved towards the injured man. "Get in touch with whoever you can. We need to get out of here," he spoke to Joe as he moved away.

Ibrahim burned with fever. They had managed to stem the flow of blood from his wounds, and now the skin around them was red with infection. He panted rapid, shallow breaths, like a dog in the heat of summer.

"I need more cold towels. Soak them all and cover him. We need to try and bring this fever down." As he spoke, Jeff looked closer at the wounds on Ibrahim's torso. He could see the curve of the individual teeth. He shuddered, as the image of the two people on the deck below flashed in his mind.

Rising, Jeff turned to Zahi. He took him by the arm and led him away. "Listen, something is going on on this ship. I don't think Ibrahim is going to make it. I'm not saying this lightly, or because I've given up, but I know how religious you all are, and if there is anything that needs to be done, or said, before you die, well…I just want you to be prepared." He placed a hand on the young officer's shoulder and gave it a squeeze. He could feel the man shaking.

"Thank you, sir," Zahi replied.

Jeff watched as the men covered Ibrahim with wet towels. The feeling of fear had grown; it no longer occupied just his stomach, but consumed every inch of his being.

CHAPTER 12

When the alarm sounded, neither Jose nor Sofia paid it much attention. They had decided to take in a movie, and were settled into the back row of the fourth, and smallest, cinema located on deck six.

A few other people seemed to share their idea, but not enough for the cinema to be classified as busy. It suited the young married could perfectly, as their lust levels continued to rise.

Both knew that their decision to watch the movie only acted to delay their returning to the room. Not because they were nervous or worried about the evening, but because they wanted to savour it, to draw it out as long as possible.

The film, a so-called thriller, turned out to be as predictable as a Disney movie. Not that it really mattered, because they were not watching much of it, anyway.

The first round of alarms startled those in the cinema, but because the movie continued playing, none paid it any real mind.

What got them moving was when the door to the theatre burst open and a crowd of screaming people ran in. They charged into the dark room and closed the door behind them.

Sofia screamed in surprise as the people flooded the room, the sound of their cries drowning out the movie.

In the darkness of the movie theatre, everything seemed amplified. Someone pushed into Sofia and sent her falling to the floor. Jose spun around and shoved the mystery attacker that pushed his wife.

"Sofia, baby, are you okay?" Jose dropped to one knee beside his wife, who was weeping quietly.

"I think…what's happening?" she asked.

"I don't know," Jose answered.

Hands clamped down on Jose's shoulders and pulled him from the floor. His feet left the ground as he was hurled through the cinema. Jose landed two rows further down, and felt his arm snap beneath him as he collided with the movie seats. He gave a cry, but above that, he heard Sofia scream.

Pulling himself to his feet, Jose leaped over the seats and reached forward for whoever had grabbed Sofia. The figure was solid and as heavy as concrete, but Jose came at him from an angle that put the figure off-balance. Jose pulled as hard as he could, and the figure tumbled backward, falling over the seats. Both Jose and the assailant fell to the floor. Cold hands clamped over Jose's face, smothering him. He struggled against the grip, but mostly against the smell. The meaty tang of blood consumed Jose's world. He couldn't breathe. The shallow breaths he managed to snatch tasted like death. Jose gagged as probing fingers tried to force their way into his mouth. He bit down hard, feeling his teeth sink through the flesh, but his attacker did not flinch.

The lights came on and the movie screen fell to black. The frantic activity in the movie theatre came into full view.

Jose found his feet in the light and pushed away from the hands that held him. He stood up and found Sofia looking at him. Blood streaked down the right-hand side of her face, flowing from a deep wound above her eyebrow. The look in her eyes made Jose tremble.

He had heard the expression "a deer caught in the headlights" before, but until that moment never fully understood what it meant. Turning his head, following Sofia's line of sight, he found himself staring at their attacker, the man who had thrown him through the room and who had caused his wife to bleed. Time stopped. The carnage unfolding around them froze.

The man standing before him was a dishevelled wreck of a human being. His hair, which at first looked like a poorly-fitted toupee, flapped on his scalp in a bloody tear, while half of his face was missing, revealing the jaw and teeth beneath.

Misty white eyes stared in their direction, while the creature swung for them, his fingers curled into claws, set in place, as if frozen.

Jose jumped, causing the man to miss the swing and stumble closer to them. The rest of the scene came back to life also, revealing the true extent of the chaos. They were not alone in the fight. The room was filled with freaks, all intent on tearing apart the movie's meagre audience.

Jose grabbed Sofia by the hand and turned to run. Ahead of them, blocking the end of the row where Jose stood, another man caught a scared teen and tore into him. Hands disappeared into the young teen's gut, and pulled his belly open with a wet tear. The teen's insides fell to the floor with a splat. The victim didn't scream. He simply stared down at the hole in his belly, and watched for a moment as his attacker shoved handfuls of bloody meat into his mouth.

The kid hit the floor, landing in a pile of his own guts. Sofia screamed, drawing the attention of the creatures nearest to them.

Leaping, Jose moved into the same row of seats as his wife. Turning back the other way, he pushed the reaching thing out of the way, sending it back another row of seats. Running, with Sofia's hand clamped within his own, Jose charged through the seats, leaving the carnage behind him. Others followed suit. Several fell, pulled back by the desperate claws of the dead.

Jose burst through the second set of exit doors into what he hoped would be the safety of the ship. What they found was blood, blood and bodies lay strewn everywhere. Whole bodies, dismembered bodies and hollowed out bodies. The voices of the injured rang out like a mournful cry. Their pleas for help lessening with each spurt of blood, with each convulsion.

The coppery musk of blood was overpowering, and the hard floor was slick with human offal.

"Help me," a middle-aged woman screamed. She reached out with both hands, pulling them away from her wounded belly. Her intestines dangled in thick purple loops, like discoloured jungle vines.

"What's happening?" Sofia asked, tears blinding her to the full extent of the horror-filled scene.

"I don't know, but come on." Jose tugged on her arm. Sofia followed, but heavily. She was shutting down.

Jose turned and pulled her into his arms. He hugged his wife in a tight embrace, shielding her from the scene. "Listen to me. We are going to be fine. We just need to get away from here. I won't let anything hurt you." Jose kissed Sofia on the cheek, one, two, three times.

"My head hurts. I'm dizzy and tired." Her voice sounded frail.

"You got hit in the head, but we will get you taken care of," Jose answered, stroking the loose strands of hair behind her ears.

Sofia looked at him, her body trembling. "Where are we going to go?"

At that moment, another alarm rang out, cutting above the sounds of the slaughter. "Ladies and gentlemen, this is Captain Joe Sheen. In light of current circumstances, I am going to have to request all passengers report to the nearest emergency collection point and await further instruction. I repeat, all passengers are to report to the nearest emergency collection point. Thank you." The voice cut out, but the instructions were clear.

"Where is that?" Sofia asked, even more panicked than before.

"I don't know…wait, this way." Jose took her hand once more and led her through the turmoil towards the observation desk.

They turned a corner and found themselves in a throng of survivors. Each was lost to their own panic, not interested in the fate of the others. As they moved, Jose saw a large man, who was still holding onto a huge double cheeseburger, shove a young woman out of his way, and into the waiting hands of a pair of the undead.

She screamed as they took equal hold and pulled on her until she was torn in two. Her body came apart like a wishbone, tearing from the point where her left shoulder connected with her neck, meaning that by the time the two halves ripped apart at the crotch, finally separating the poor thing, one creature had a decidedly larger portion than the other.

Sofia vomited and fell to the floor. Jose caught her, pulling her into his arms. He moved forward as best could, his own adrenaline resources running on empty.

They saw the bodies littered through the fast food court, their remains scattered with fries and burger buns. The dead were everywhere, on their knees, faces buried in the deliciously greasy treats. Savage jaws tore thick strips of succulent flesh from bones, smacking them down with a crunch that made Jose think of eating raw celery.

Turning his back on the scene, Jose focused on leading Sofia and himself safely through the sea of fleeing bodies. He noticed that the brutes who had shoved people out of their way had already made it outside, while those who suffered from their selfish actions were already being digested in the bellies of the reanimated dead.

They moved past the playground, and the cries of those trapped inside made Jose stop. One of the viewing windows was smeared with blood from the inside, and hungry, high-pitched growls echoed down the slide, which spilled onto a mat along the edge of the deck's main corridor.

Sofia groaned in his arms, and Jose found his momentum again.

They reached the observation deck and stepped out into the night. The cries of those inside fell mute, when suddenly, not moments after they emerged through them, the doors were pushed closed by two blood-covered, terrified looking members of the crew.

Those trapped on the inside began to hammer on the glass. It was a short-lived concern, for the dead picked them off like fish in a barrel. It was a mercy when the spilled blood from their torn out throats obscured the view from out on the deck.

Bodies filled the small deck space. Everybody huddled close together, forming small groups at first, but soon they became larger, fear being the glue that bound them. Nobody spoke, everybody whimpered, lost in his or her own suffering, but drowning in the knowledge that those around them had suffered just as much, if not more.

Their group continued to merge and gel; the murmurs became cries and whimpers, questions and questions, unanswerable questions. Jose walked Sofia away from the group, which was stifling in its closeness. The pair leaned against the railing, hands interlocked. Neither spoke, as there was nothing either could say.

Everybody was too absorbed to see the injured among them, and nobody thought to separate themselves from the bitten.

When the dead rose, there was nowhere left for the living to run.

CHAPTER 13

Shouts and screams filled the corridor, and while the siren blared, Derrick moved back into his room. His wife was awake, sitting bolt upright in bed. She was shaking and pale, her eyes wide with fear.

"What's going on?" she asked.

"I don't know, but come on, let's move it to the emergency point. You heard the captain, we need to move." Derrick stuttered. He was scared, but knew that he was the man of the family, and it was his job to keep them safe.

Carol got out of bed and dressed, while Derrick woke his son. Michael woke with bleary eyes, oblivious to the drama that was unfolding around them.

"Dad?" he asked, his voice sluggish.

"It's ok, but we need to leave the room for a little while." Derrick said, not sure how to deliver the news. His mind was going a hundred miles an hour, in every possible direction.

Michael got out of bed as the second blast of the siren sounded.

"Come here, Michael, stay close to me," Carol called, and Michael scurried over to his mother.

Derrick moved to the bed to wake Celia. He called her but got no response. Reaching to shake her, Derrick found his daughter cold and unresponsive. His brain failed to compute what had happened. He continued to shake Celia, calling her name over and over, growing more exasperated at her refusal to listen to him.

Without warning, his grip broke and Derrick fell to the floor, sobbing and wailing as he clutched the bed covers in white-knuckled fists.

"No, my baby, my little girl," he repeated over and over, until spit and tears drowned out his words and reduced him to nothing more than a groaning puddle on the floor.

Carol moved toward the bed, terrified and confused. She reached for her daughter, and while her heartbreak was just as severe, her reaction was to sit on the bed and pull Celia's death-stiffened frame into her arms. She sat there, rocking back and forth, stoking her daughter's hair and kissing her forehead. She never said a word.

The silence was deafening. Derrick could no longer bring himself to utter a sound, his throat raw. Michael stood in the middle of the room, alone, a spreading patch of wetness on his trousers. His body was stiff with fear. His face contorted with grief he could not bring himself to let loose. He couldn't even breathe, let alone make a sound.

After a silence that seemed to last a thousand lifetimes, Carol began to howl. She screamed at the top of her voice, drowning out the calls and shrieks from the rest of the ship. She wailed uncontrollably, and thrashed on the bed. The reaction brought Derrick to his feet. In that moment, he knew he needed his wife, and that she needed him.

Derrick stood up and wiped his eyes, his tears hot against his hands. Yet, he could not deny wiping them away felt good.

Lowering his hands, Derrick received a face full of blood for his troubles. Falling backwards into one of the armchairs, he looked at the bed and saw Celia lying in her mother's arms, blood spurting up into the air above them. Carol's eyes were wide open, a scream dead in her throat, as her daughter's teeth continued to ravage her flesh.

Derrick got to his feet and reached out for Celia, an instinctive reaction. The cool stiffness of her body was a shock. Celia flinched, spinning around on her father, tearing away her mother's left breast in the process. Celia growled at her father, while chewing on her mother's tit, which dangled from her mouth by the nipple. She rolled from the bed and approached her father.

"Celia…baby…" Derrick tried to speak, but he could not find the words. He body was shutting down, he could feel it.

"Leave him alone," Michael shrieked, running to push his sister to one side.

They had often fought over the years, but it was always Celia who played the aggressor, and rarely did their fights get physical, or any more physical than your standard sibling squabbles at such young ages. Celia growled at her brother, her white eyes twitching restlessly in their sockets. She leaped and landed on top of Michael, who somehow managed to push his sister up and over him. Celia fell against the main chest of drawers and mini-bar unit with a heavy crunch. Her shoulder was caught beneath her and gave an audible pop.

Rather the crying, she just rolled over and got back to her feet, her left arm hanging uselessly at her side. She approached Michael again, and again he kicked out, forcing her back another step.

Turning around, Michael took in the scene, his father stunned on the chair, his mother slowly sinking into a pool of blood on the bed, and his sister coming at him like a beast. Michael saw the door, and ran, oblivious to the problems throughout the ship. He heard his father call him, but refused to listen. He ran, yanked open the door and disappeared into the hall.

The growls came through louder now, and Celia turned toward them, following her brother out of the door.

Derrick moved to follow. He heard Michael scream, and heard the way his voice fell suddenly silent. His world broke and he fell onto the bed.

"Derrick?" Carol wheezed. "I'm sorry."

"What…no, no, don't you dare do that." Derrick started. "Don't you dare!"

Derrick got up from the bed and moved toward the door. The scent of blood was overwhelming and shadows danced on the walls. Peering into the hallway, Derrick saw people running in, slipping and sliding through the corridor. Behind him, something growled.

Derrick turned and came face to face with an older man, his chest length beard matted with blood, a severed finger caught in the long whiskers. Derrick cried out and jumped back, colliding with the doorframe. Pain exploded in his head as the man lunged for him. Cold, dead fingers closed around his shirt and yanked with enough force to tear the cloth. Derrick wrenched himself free and disappeared back into the room. He slammed the door shut, crushing the man's reaching arm. The bone broke with a snap, and black blood spurted from the squashed flesh. The door didn't close fully, and the arm didn't stop reaching, and so Derrick opened the door and slammed it shut again, and again, three times over he slammed the door, crushing the limb until it came away in a jagged mess of pulped meat. The door closed and Derrick fell to the floor. His body tensed, as if somebody kicked him in the nuts. His stomach ached and twisted into a knot.

"Derrick," the voice called from the bed.

Crawling, thick strings of spit hanging from his lips, Derrick moved to his wife. Her skin was pale, the large tear in her chest still pumping blood, but it was clear that there was not much left to lose.

"Oh god, what's going on...I...I don't understand." Derrick wept into his wife's arms, not noticing that it was too late. Carol slipped away, and he was left hugging a corpse.

Derrick did not know how long he lay there before he realized his wife was no longer breathing, but it was not long enough. He didn't understand what was happening, but he knew what he had seen. He knew that it would not be long before his wife started to move again, and when she did, she would be just as hungry as his Celia was.

He rolled off the bed and fell to the floor. His thoughts turned to his children, his babies. The devil had taken hold of the ship, and tore his family apart in the space of a few minutes.

The cruise was supposed to have helped them heal; instead, it proved to be their undoing.

Derrick hauled himself from the floor and into the armchair. He sat in silence, too tired to cry, too broken to move. He watched and waited, knowing the moment would soon come.

It started with a twitch. Not much more than a single gentle spasm in the leg, but it built, and soon Carol's corpse was growling and shaking. Motion coming back to the still-warm body. The joints still supple, the effects of death having not yet taken hold. Her head shook, and her eyes opened. The scent of living flesh caught her attention. Carol turned her head, and her white eyes seemed to bore holes through Derrick. He swallowed hard as she opened her mouth.

Rolling on the bed, Carol pulled herself over the soft mattress and fell to the floor. She was no more than a few feet away from where Derrick sat, but he didn't move. He couldn't.

Snarling and thrashing, her movements growing with intensity as her second life took full control of her body, Carol pulled herself to her feet and regarded the man in the chair. Any lingering thoughts of recognition or conscience Derrick held was washed away. There was nothing but hunger and hate in the creature that had once been his wife.

"Do it," he spat, exhausted. "Eat me."

The undead Carol collapsed onto the chair, unmoved by the easy nature of her meal. Her cold arms were stiff against Derrick, pinning him in place. Her head cocked to the side, and her lips parted as if she intended to steal a kiss. As she leaned in, Derrick began to tremble. His resolve crumbled and he found himself resisting.

Derrick pushed back with every ounce of strength he could muster. Slowly, pushing away inch-by-inch, Derrick fought for his freedom. The greater the distance between them, the more he wept, and the worse he felt. Derrick wanted to die. He had lost everything, yet he could not bring himself to take that step. He was too much of a coward.

"I'm sorry," he wept as he shoved his wife backward, sending her crashing into the wall.

Carol shook off the impact and came back at Derrick, who was back-peddling toward the door. Carol moved slowly, but with only limited room to work. Derrick needed to think fast.

He threw open the door to the wardrobe, sending it crashing into his wife's face. Her nose and lips shattered, but she did nothing more than growl harder.

"Carol...honey...it's me," Derrick whimpered, pushing away at his wife as she neared him.

His shoves became more forceful, the final one causing Carol to stumble backward. She fell, but not before her nails tore a deep gouge along Derrick's forearm. The scent of blood only served to further agitate Carol as she clawed her way back to her feet and fell toward Derrick. They crumbled to the floor in a heap, Carol's teeth snapping at Derrick's throat.

Carol mounted Derrick in the struggle, leaving him with no leverage to push her away. Switching to a single-arm defence, he sacrificed space for a free arm. Groping, while the hungry teeth snarled less than an inch away from his skin, Derrick prayed.

A thick trail of spit dangled from Carol's lips. Her body writhed as she tried to get a better position. Derrick's hand found something and wrapped around it. He didn't know what it was, but it was solid, and his only hope. Swinging, he slapped his wife with a shoehorn. It had little effect as a single strike, but in his final moments, Derrick discovered that he was perfectly competent to fight like a young girl and so started slapping his wife in a flurried attack, which managed to give him the necessary momentum to turn her over. Rolling through, they ended with in reversed positions.

Derrick looked around and saw the iron hanging on the wall in the cupboard. He yanked it free and straddled his wife, holding the weapon above his head. He stared at Carol, her image hazy through his tears. Her face was torn and bloody. She snarled and scratched at him.

"Carol, listen to me, sweetheart, please," Derrick begged.

Carol snatched at him, scratching a tear in his trousers, the nails raking over his flesh.

"I'm sorry," Derrick wailed as he brought the iron home on his wife's skull.

He tried to stop, to pull back, but all he managed to do was extend the process, denting Carol's face in three places before he finally followed through with a swing that burst her head like a grape.

Derrick dropped the gore-encrusted iron and fell atop his wife. "I'm sorry, I forgive you...I forgive you." He repeated the phrase over and over until his throat was raw. He hugged his wife's corpse long into the night, sleeping beside her one last time, until the blood had set in his hair, and grief had penetrated him to the bone.

CHAPTER 14

Eric and Tara left his room in a swarm of fleeing bodies. Everything happened so fast. They were surrounded by shrieks and cries, but the throng of people seemed to push them in every possible direction.

Eric could hear the captain's voice over the loudspeaker, a recording no doubt, because each repetition of the order to meet at an emergency location was delivered with the same amount of fear. Eric focused himself by holding onto Tara's hand. He had no idea what was building between them, but at that point in time, she grounded him, and he did not plan on letting her go.

The emergency collection point on their deck was a small area of open deck which could only be accessed through emergency doors, meaning it was not used at any point during the voyage. The area was not designed to have an entire floor gathered there. It was for a quick exit point.

Pandemonium erupted in the hallway, and other than the dead body by their door, there had been nothing to explain the direct cause. They ran with the crowd, but Eric realized it served no purpose the moment he noticed where they were headed.

"This area is full. We will need to move up to the other decks," a voice called out. A member of the crew appeared, a tiny looking man who raised his hands and expected it to be enough to stop the crushing wave of bodies.

Shouts and protestations filled the corridor.

"I'm sorry. We can take the elevator to the upper levels. I would suggest we head to the Lido deck. There is plenty of space there, and we can lock down the doors," the small man continued. The crowd tried to force its way through, but he showed conviction greater than his size, and refused to move.

One by one, people turned and hurried toward the lifts.

Eric and Tara squeezed into the first lift that arrived. Another member of the crew stood inside, operating the controls. He was of a similar build to the first man, but had a thick, well-trimmed beard covering the lower half of his face. Regardless of the facial hair, the man still looked utterly terrified.

The elevator was over-crowded and groaned as it rose. Eric looked around, trying to find the board that confirmed the same numbers and weight limit. He knew they were over it. All he found was Tara's eyes staring at him. He squeezed her hand gently, and wished they could find the space to move even closer to one another.

The elevator reached its destination, and the bearded crewmember began to issue some instructions on where they were to go. It was standard operating procedure, being implemented under circumstances nobody ever dared consider.

He didn't talk for long, however. The moment the lift doors opened, hands grabbed his beard and tore it free from his face in a single yank. The skin came away too, leaving nothing but the blood-drenched bones of the man's lower jaw. More hands appeared, pulling the man backward, where he was swiftly torn apart.

Eric pulled Tara and broke into a run. One of the first people out of the elevator, he had a few precious moments of space. He saw the doors along the wall which led to the deck, but he pulled Tara past them and continued running over the deck.

"Where are you going?" she asked, scared.

"Outside, but those doors will be a mad rush," Eric answered, out of breath.

Tara remained quiet, sprinting. They reached the double doors and the end of the corridor and charged through them. They came out onto a small side deck, which fed the main area.

It was empty, and nobody else seemed to have cottoned on to their plan. A creature in the bloody remains of a crewmember's uniform, clearly a woman at one point in time, crashed against the doors. They rattled but did not give.

Eric stood and stared at her for a while. Her pale skin, the white eyes that still moved in their sockets, as if fully able to focus on people. Eric shuddered as the creature began biting at the glass, somehow convinced that it could eat through the door to get to the fresh meat on the other side.

"Here, help me with this," Eric said, responding to the gentle hand that fell on his shoulder.

Together he and Tara managed to move one of the stored secondary life raft capsules from its holdings on the inner wall and onto the deck. When placed lengthways, it just fit, blocking the door, and stopping anything from using them.

"We just locked people inside," Tara said, backing away from the door as if it were poison.

"Don't think of that. There are other doors. Nobody was using this one," Eric offered. He felt the same heavy feeling in his heart, but he believed in survival.

Alone on the deck, the silence was less enjoyable than either would have thought. They fell onto the nearest bench and sat looking out at the night sky.

"You know, if you take away the dead trying to eat us, I would say this was a pretty good first day," Tara spoke, the dry wit in her voice catching Eric by surprise.

"You know what? It ranks up there in both lists, good and bad," he answered, wrapping his arm around Tara, pulling her close to him.

They sat together for some time, only moving toward the Lido deck when they felt ready for it. They could hear the cries and murmured appeals for answers, and felt no immediate inclination to join the masses.

"Excuse me; it is not safe out here. I need to ask you to join the rest of the people on the main deck area," a nervous voice spoke.

Eric looked over at him and saw the blood that covered his uniform. "Are you sure it is safe over there?"

"Please," the man repeated, desperate.

"Come on, let's go." Tara made the decision, and rose from the bench.

The deck was busy with everybody crowded into large groups. Eric looked around and saw they had blocked every door and exit on the deck. They were trapped, and he was not sure if that was a good thing.

Nobody turned to pay attention to their late arrival. Nobody paid attention to anything. From their detached position, Eric noticed the crew had shown the wherewithal to separate people into two basic groups, the injured and not. Eric saw people with missing limbs and deep lacerations all over their bodies. He wondered how many people had been bitten. After a lifetime of reading comics and horror novels, Eric thought he understood enough to know how it worked.

The other thing Eric noticed was that while the crew had acted fast to separate people, they did not appear to have put a lot of thought into what happened after. There was no clear leader on the deck, and all it would take was a single event to bring everything crashing down around them.

In the middle of the herd, someone cried out, and within a moment, everybody understood why. A dead man fell from the sky, dropping over the railing from the deck. The body exploded with a wet slapping sound, but it served a purpose. It alerted everybody to the fact that the dead were everywhere, while instilling a fresh wave of panic. The dead on the second level of the Lido deck had been forgotten. With the doors left unsecured, the dead poured through. Some people reacted, trying to block the stairs with sun loungers and anything else they could get their hands on. Others screamed and turned to run, but they were crammed together like sheep.

Eric watched as several people moved away from the group, skirting the large main pool area. They walked to the railings, scaled them and promptly jumped. Nobody noticed, or, at least, the shock of their suicide no longer carried any weight given all that had transpired.

Eric saw them, he felt for them, and refused to sit back and allow it to happen.

CHAPTER 15

"Sir..." a voice called across the bridge.

Both Joe and Jeff turned around.

"You need to see this," the same voice continued. The older man was an experienced member of the crew. He had already been on board when the captain and his XO arrived. His name was Nour, and even in the short time they had known each other, Joe believed Nour to be a man he could trust.

The two men moved forward, passing the unconscious Ibrahim, whose body lie draped in blood-soaked towels. His body gave off a terrible odour, which permeated the air of the bridge like that of rancid meat.

"What is it, Nour?" Joe asked, placing his hand on the man's shoulder as he spoke.

"It's...it's the passengers, sir, look." Nour pointed through the main bridge window and down to the deck. The Lido deck was largely shrouded in darkness, but the ship's lights cast enough of a glow over the edge of the deck, which meant they all got to watch the scene unfold.

In groups of as many as ten or fifteen, the passengers climbed the ship's railings, only to send themselves hurtling towards the ocean.

"Maybe they think they can swim to safety?" Nour offered.

"No, the fall alone will kill them instantly. They know that, but they would rather die than come back again," Joe answered, his eyes fixed on the scene, no matter how hard he tried to divert his gaze.

"I hope they find peace, my friend." Nour turned away, his cheeks wet with tears.

Jeff stood beside Joe. He said nothing; he just watched, studying everything.

"What are you thinking, Joe?" the captain asked.

"I think we are royally fucked. Some kind of unholy hell has broken loose on this ship, and even if we turn around now, we will never make it back to the shore." Jeff turned to look his captain in the eye.

"You think they spread that fast?" Joe was horrified at the thought.

"No, not everybody. I mean they won't let us dock. We physically won't be able to make it to the shore. You see what is going on down there. No way that they will take a chance on this making it onto dry land." Jeff turned his head back to the window. He saw a figure by the railings waving his arms and pulling people back down. He saved those he could reach, but several got back to their feet and threw themselves over at a run.

"They wouldn't," Joe replied.

"They would sooner blow this ship up than risk it hitting land. I know, Joe; I've been on the other side. Not with the dead waking, but with other real threats. Collateral damage, that is what we are now."

"That's a bit bleak, man." Joe was taken aback by Jeff's comments, but what hurt more was knowing the truth behind them.

"The world can be a shitty place." Jeff nodded, watching as a mother leaped from the fence, having kicked away at the man trying to stop her. She jumped with her children in her arms, clinging on to her for love and support.

"Ibrahim," one of the crewmembers called.

The bridge seemed to turn in one fluid motion to stare at the injured man. Only, he was no longer lying on the floor. The figure had vanished, leaving behind it the bloody towel and a streaked smear over the floor.

"Watch out," Jeff called, but it was too late. Ibrahim grabbed Issam from behind and sank his teeth into the back of the man's head, tearing a great slice of hair and scalp free. Issam fell to the floor, screaming in pain as Ibrahim fell upon him, chomping into his flesh like a pig at a swill trough.

"Everybody move," Jeff called out, pulling his gun free from his trousers. He took aim and fired at Ibrahim. The bullet pierced his shoulder, knocking him off balance. Issam was dead, his flesh chewed away to reveal the spine beneath, as good as separating the head from the body.

Ibrahim rolled over and hauled himself to his feet. The crew on the bridge ran in blind panic, ruining Jeff's chances of getting a clean shot. He fired anyway, missing wildly.

"Joe, Nour, get these people back. I need them clear, now." Jeff ordered, striding through the bodies, crossing the bridge. He walked with purpose. He reached Ibrahim and swung a large fist. He connected with the dead man's head. He never saw it coming, for he was too busy feasting on the flesh of Ahmad's leg.

Ibrahim fell to the floor, snarling and snapping, but was met by the short barrel of Jeff's pistol.

"I'm sorry," Jeff spoke as he pulled the trigger.

Ibrahim's head exploded out the back, showering the floor with a splattering of skin, bone and sticky globs of brain tissue.

The bridge was a bloody mess; bodies lay on the floor with chunks taken from various places on their body. Issam, Zahi, Ahmad and Saad, the youngest member of the crew, had all been bitten. Only Issam was already dead, but the others knew that their fates were sealed.

"What do we do, Jeff?" Joe asked from the corner. He was pale and sweating.

"Well, first things first, we try and stop that chopper from landing." Jeff said, pointing out of the bridge window where he could see the lights of the approaching trauma helicopter.

"I'll take care of that," Joe began, but when he picked up the receiver to hail the helo, Jeff stopped him.

"What can we tell them? Don't land, the dead have risen and we are all doomed. No, we need to let them land, give them someone and then get them off the ship again." Jeff was thinking on his feet, a plan forming in his head. He didn't like it. He didn't like any of it.

"What do you have in mind?" Joe asked.

Jeff didn't give an answer, but turned around, picked a target, and shot the uninjured man in the leg.

The crewmember, whose name Jeff did not know, and after that moment, did not want to know, fell to the floor, screaming. His hands clamped at his leg, squeezing, making the blood flow thicker.

"Don't squeeze it. The helo is coming in now. We will get you on board, and they will patch you up. I'm a good shot; I know what I'm talking about," Jeff spoke as he dropped to the floor and tied a rough tourniquet.

"Joe, you stay here, wait for the chopper to leave and then turn this ship. We need to head toward land," Jeff instructed, talking to a silenced room.

"But I thought you said we couldn't make land?" Joe asked, knowing his XO had a plan, but confused as to what it was.

"I said they would not let us make land. I don't plan on asking permission. Wait for that helo to be gone, and then move us to the coast, away from a harbour." Jeff turned and pointed at three uninjured crewmembers. They shrank away under his gaze. "You three, I need you to take the injured and quarantine them somewhere. Lock them away in the mess hall, anything. Just make sure they are secure. Nour, I need to you come with me. We need to bring this man down to that helo and get them away before they can realize anything is wrong."

Nobody argued with Jeff, nobody dared. They all knew his history.

"That chopper is coming in fast, my friend. How can we get down to them in time?" Nour spoke up.

"You can use the escape elevator. It runs all the way down to the lower levels. You can stop at the first floor, by security. Then it is just two floors up to the helipad," Joe offered, as he punched in coordinates to move the ship.

"That'll work." Jeff nodded to himself. "Keep this ship steady."

"We need to turn now. This whole thing won't be any use if they see the pandemonium on the decks." Joe was quick to answer.

"Shit, we need more than lady luck for this," Jeff answered, looking around the room. "It's now or never. Let's move."

Moving their patient into the small emergency elevator was easy—the idea that the man was going to be offered a way off the ship went some way to easing his pain and speeding up his movements.

None of the men spoke as they rode the elevator down to the security deck. Jeff was not sure where it would come out. He was happy when the doors opened to put them within the security office, behind the electronic locked doors.

What he did not expect was the armed team of terrified guards that spun around just as the doors opened.

Jeff threw himself to the floor, as did Nour. A wall of bullets pummelled the chest of the injured man, decimating his flesh, rendering it a bubbling slab of meat.

"Hold your fire, hold your fucking fire," Jeff roared, rolling out of the lift to meet the men. He put three of them on the floor, nursing a range of injuries before he caught control of himself.

"Fucking shit! What have you assholes done?" Jeff roared.

"Sorry, sir." Captain Rasheed stepped forward, noticing the uniform Jeff wore. "We didn't know."

"You didn't know. Well know this, asshole. You may well have just killed us all," Jeff snarled and with one punch put the captain on his ass.

"Calm down, my friend." Nour moved in front of Jeff, breaking his gaze on the security staff. "They are scared, we are all scared. These men are not military. We do not have time for fighting like this." Nour placed his hands on Jeff's shoulders. He felt the man tense, and after a few seconds, felt him relax.

"You're right, we need a plan."

CHAPTER 17

"I see the ship," Hasan Assi said as he tipped his helicopter into a tight turn.

It was dark out, but the hulking shadow of the cruise ship was hard to miss.

"The landing pad is on the stern, so I'm going to swing us around the front of the ship and come around from the back," Hasan spoke to the paramedic who sat in the main cabin of the search and rescue helicopter.

"Ok, just tell me when we land," Mohammad Tamim spoke through a clenched jaw.

"We are almost there, my friend. This trip was nothing; imagine doing this during a storm, with gunfire coming at you from all directions." Hasan laughed when he heard the young paramedic groan.

A serious incident meant their hospital was already stretched to its maximum capacity. As a result, it had fallen upon the young paramedic to make the trip, and the transition from four wheels to four rotor blades did not agree with him.

It was only his second trip in the helicopter, and the first time had not been a pleasant experience for him, or any of the people involved. Hasan on the other hand, being an ex-military man, had flown combat missions and seen things he vowed never to talk about. Thanks to his training, he knew how to stay cool and controlled when under pressure. Yet, when they swung around the front of the ship, a feeling of dread washed over him.

"Looks like they are having quite the party," Tamim spoke. Their sudden proximity to something more grounded than the helo seemed to liven his spirits.

"Yeah, looks like it," Hasan answered, his eyes fixed on the gathered crowd. There was something about it all that bothered him, but he had no idea what it was. Not until it was too late.

From the bridge, Captain Joe Sheen watched the helicopter approach, and cursed when he saw it turn his way, swinging around the front of the ship. He shouted at the pilot to keep going, causing the three remaining bridge crew members to jump.

The others were busy moving the bodies. The injured men moved under their fruition, walking albeit begrudgingly into their designated holding area. The dead, however, were a different story. Especially the ones that started to squirm in their grip as life returned to their bodies.

The helo rounded the ship and disappeared from view. Joe hoped that Jeff made it to the deck in time. He figured he would know either way soon enough.

Hasan placed the chopper gently and neatly onto the centre of the helipad. Tamim was already unstrapped and halfway out the door.

Shutting down the main rotor blades, but leaving the bird ready for an easy power up, Hasan got out and moved to help the medic. They grabbed the bags and prepared the stretcher when the doors opened.

They turned around, startled by what sounded like screams. Three people charged toward them. Each one covered in blood. It looked like a scene from the Carrie remake, had the prom been held out at sea.

"What's happened here?" Tamim began to ask, but the charging passengers ignored his question and pushed him out of the way to clamber into the helicopter.

"Who here is hurt? What happened?" Tamim tried again, but nobody answered him.

Screams rang out from inside the ship as the doors opened and a second group of people charged out. They ran towards the helicopter. This group was far more vocal, shouting and screaming about monsters and people being eaten alive.

Tamim turned his focus to the patients. He needed something to deal with, something physical. Hasan was different. While he did not know cause of their panic, he knew enough to understand they needed to get off the ship.

"Get in the chopper. We need to leave," he called to everybody that was already piling into the cabin.

"There are others in there," one man turned to speak. He was an older man, dressed in a bloody and torn dinner suit. He had a wild look to him, as if he had been put through an intense day of assault-based field training.

"We don't have time for them. We need to leave. We can come back with others." Hasan pushed Tamim back towards the chopper, as good as lifting him into the cabin.

The rotors whirred and the bird took to the sky just before Jeff and Nour appeared on the deck, Captain Rasheed and his depleted security team just behind them.

"We're too late," Nour remarked, watching as the helicopter disappeared into the night.

"Then I guess you have a call to make, don't you?" Jeff didn't look at Nour as he spoke; he didn't need to.

"You knew. How?" Nour asked, his voice flat, refusing to give away the shock he felt.

"I knew something," Jeff answered, now turning to face the man. "I didn't know what, and still don't. I do, however, understand what will happen if this issue gets onto the mainland, and what will happen when the military hear about what is on this ship. So either way, we are royally fucked. I don't know whose side you are on, but we are against the wall, and I am hoping you are fighting for the right team." Jeff held Nour's gaze.

"I will make the call, but what good will it do? The weapon has been deployed," Nour asked, his cool demeanour still not showing the slightest sign of cracks.

"We will cross that bridge next. First we need to buy us some time. Make the call." Jeff turned and walked away, leaving the man standing on his own on the helipad. Inside the door, the roughly assembled team of Captain Rasheed and his two remaining living, uninjured security offers stood on guard, ready to shoot any undead figure that came their way.

On board the helicopter, Tamim was busy trying to calm the crowd and assess the extent of their injuries. The bird was overcrowded, and as a result, they were flying heavy and sluggish. Most of the wounds seemed either superficial or Tamim was able to patch people up well enough to get them to the hospital. It was the stories they were telling that worried him the most.

From the cockpit, Hasan also listened. Everybody spoke individually, not bothered by the people around him, and yet every story was the same, identical down to the letter. Something was on board the ship, and it was killing passengers.

The cruise ship was behind them now, its lights fading like the memory of a bad dream upon waking. Yet he had the feeling that had washed over him when he saw the crowded decks, refusing to let go. It clamped onto his soul and try as he might, Hasan could not shake it free.

Something streaked through the air to their left. Hasan turned his head, but did not even have the chance to scream. The missile came straight at them, and within moments of being launched, it crashed into the moving helo and those inside it were blown apart.

"Was that your guys?" Jeff asked as Nour appeared back on the deck.

"No, that was somebody else. We are not alone on this ship," Nour spoke, but his words trailed away as Captain Rasheed turned his gun on them both.

"It was not supposed to happen like this, my friends. I'm sorry, truly I am." He looked at his two other officers. "Take them."

The two men advanced on Jeff and Nour, leaving the third member of the team confused. He looked around, watching for the approaching dead. Captain Rasheed shot him in the back of the head.

"You gentlemen are going to come with me. If you don't behave, I will feed you to the creatures that are running amok on board this ship." It was not so much his words that got the two men moving, but a mixture of the M16 he was holding and the approaching group of the undead, that, having picked up on their scent, now came stumbling their way.

CHAPTER 18

Robert sat on the floor of the small room, his back against the door, holding it with all of his weight, even though nothing and nobody was trying to get in from the other side.

He could not tell how long he had been there. Ever since he boarded the ship, life had gotten steadily worse. Time lost all meaning. He understood that. The only thing that was important was survival. To stay alive and not get eaten by the undead.

He understood that he couldn't hide in one place forever. He needed to move, to find a safe place where he could escape. To do that, he would need a weapon, something to help keep him alive. Spying a broom in the far corner, Robert scrambled away from the door, grabbed the broom and yanked the handle free. The main pole was thick and sturdy. Robert knew it would not last forever, but it gave him something, and he felt braver for having it in his hands.

The sounds of panic no longer resonated from the hallway, but Robert knew that meant nothing. They were on a boat in the middle of the ocean. The problem could not have gone far.

He swallowed hard, and opened the door. The hallway was empty, or, well, it was empty of life. Bodies littered the floor, their carcasses torn open and flung aside. Blood flowed over the floor like a river. Half-eaten organs lay everywhere, while stands of bloated intestines lay strewn around like trip wires, waiting to snare any unlucky soul that stood on them.

Robert moved slowly, looking around with every step he took. The growl of the dead echoed through the hallway, a constant threat and reminder that danger was everywhere.

Still on the eleventh deck, Robert didn't want to chance moving back outside. Instead, he moved down toward the gym area. What he wanted was to go back to his room and hide. He wanted to find the captain and force them to return to the harbour. He wanted to grab a lifeboat and escape. He wanted everything, and nothing. His mind was exploding, his head ached, and nothing made sense anymore.

The gym was ahead of him, the glass walls shattered, the hallway filled with weight plates. The split-open corpse of a muscle-bound man sat blocking the door to the stairwell. Robert tried to move him, but could not shift the man's bulk.

"Hello, is anybody there?" a voice came from inside the gym.

Robert froze. He doubted that the dead could talk, but he also doubted that he was the only one interested in the owner of the voice.

"Please, don't leave me alone," whoever the owned the voice spoke again.

"You're not alone," Robert answered, his voice carrying through the quiet halls. He cursed himself, and hurried inside the gym, stepping through the broken glass. The floor crunched and snapped beneath his feet, and he flinched at every sound.

More bodies filled the gym than Robert had anticipated. Among the carnage, he saw muscular limbs torn from similarly strong bodies as if they were made of paper and plastic.

Bodies sat dead in the equipment, trapped in place by leg rests and good form. Throats had been ripped apart, and clearly seemed to be the undead consumption spot of choice.

Somebody moved on the floor. Eyes turned in his direction, and that was when Robert realized they were still alive, either clinging on through sheer willpower, or dying at such a slow rate that their second life was starting before the first had been fully snuffed out.

"Hello?" Robert called.

"Hello, help me. I'm over here, in the back," the tiny voice called.

Of course you are, Robert thought to himself. He moved through the gym, which followed the standard set-up style. Stepping over bodies, and kicking the stray limb out of the way, he approached the free weight section. One corpse lay pinned beneath a heavily weighted bar. Something had torn his throat out mid-set. The weights had crashed down with enough force to cut into his skin, cracking the ribs and lodging in his sternum.

"Where are you?" Robert asked again, whispering.

"I'm here," the voice replied. He was close. Turning to move toward the far corner, he saw movement.

Robert hurried to her.

The girl was lying on the floor, trapped beneath a pile of weights. Her leg was broken, crushed by the falling equipment.

"What happened?" he asked, staring at the weights, wondering if he could, or rather, should, move them.

"I was trapped, they came at me, and well, I managed to drop a weight on one of them, but then everything else fell. My leg is broken. I can't move." The girl, who could not have been very long out of her teens wept, but her eyes remained dry; she had no more tears left to shed.

Robert looked around, and saw the zombie she had killed. A twenty-five-kilogram plate rested where its head should have been. What remained of its brains leaked around the edges of the weight in a sticky pool of goo.

"Let me see what I can do." Robert turned his attention to the weights.

Moving the first few was easy, but once he reached the lower ones, those tacky with blood, he slowed. He needed to think more about which one to move. A shard of bone protruded through not only the girl's skin, but also the centre of the under most plate. That would have to be moved last.

The girl cried out as Robert lifted a ten-kilogram plate from her upper thigh. A spurt of blood shot into the air.

"Shit," he growled, throwing the weight with a loud clatter. He placed both his hands over the spurting wound, trying to seal the gap as best he could, but it was no use. The girl bled out in a matter of moments. He could feel it, the power of the spurts, and the thump of her heart steadily ebb away beneath his hands.

"I'm sorry," he said, wiping the tears from his eyes with a blood soaked hand.

Robert stood up. He needed to move fast. He could hear the commotion growing back out on the deck.

Swapping the broom handle for a slightly meatier handle from the nearest weight station, Robert hurried from the gym and back onto the deck. Two undead figures stood crouched over a corpse at the far end, but they seemed too engrossed in their meal to notice him. Slipping through the shattered glass window, Robert moved to the outside. It was not ideal, but it would allow him to skirt back around the creatures, cut the corner of the deck and get out of there.

Outside, the full scale of the situation echoed around him. Terror filled the air, along with something else. The steady beat of the helicopter increased until the machine flew low over the top of the ship.

Robert watched it fly overhead and for a moment allowed himself to believe they could escape. A few moments later, there was a streak of light, and the helicopter was nothing but a ball of burning flame.

Robert spun around, the shot that took out the chopper coming from on the ship. He was certain about it. The streak of light had been accelerating and rising at a steep angle. Not to mention the rumble of the shot rolled across the ship like thunder striking overhead.

"What the hell is happening?" Robert asked aloud. Nobody answered, other than the growl of an undead beast that lumbered its way toward him.

Robert strode toward the creature, raising the heavy metal bar as he went. The bar came crushing down on the dead man's head, caving in his skull. Three quick, heavy strikes hollowed the head out like a bowl. Robert walked away, not looking back as the dead man fell to the floor, down permanently this time.

The *Ocean Princess* was a ship of death, and he would not add to its numbers, not without a fight. Moving over the deck, he was longer able to pick out the body of the first victim, the woman who had called to him for help from the running track. Too many bodies littered the deck.

Robert couldn't save her, and he couldn't help the young woman in the gym. In that instant, Robert realized that while he may not be able to save everybody, he could certainly take down as many of the undead second-lifers as he could.

Robert knew that there were plenty of people up on the Lido deck. He could hear their screams. That was only one deck, which meant he could take the stairs and be among them in no time.

He also reasoned that if that was the case, then at least they had each other, and they were as safe as possible. What about the others, the people trapped in the lower decks, the cabins and the like? Those separated from the rest of the ship. For them, the odds of surviving seemed infinitely less, so Robert reasoned they needed his help the most.

Robert walked past the stairs and headed to the lift. He didn't know where to start, and so went down as low as the lift would allow.

CHAPTER 19

Eric had no idea how long he spent pulling people from the ledge, but after a time everybody stopped. He was under no impression that it was his effort that stopped them, but he managed to save several innocent people, and that counted for something, at least.

The panic began to settle as the undead withdrew, distracted by something else, some fresher meat. Eric guessed that somewhere around six or seven hundred people made it to the Lido deck. He now put that number at less than half. The rest having either been torn apart or leaped to their deaths. He could understand their decision, but his faith would not allow him to stand by and watch it happen. Eric deduced that the other decks were still swarming with people who no doubt made easier targets than those barricaded onto the Lido deck.

Tara was still by his side. She also tried joining in his effort to help stop several people from jumping. They soon learned that some could not be stopped, no matter how hard they tried to convince them, or pull them free.

The explosion changed everything. People ran. They spread out, charging in all directions, screaming and shouting. Several claimed that it was a bomb, and that the boat was under attack. Others simply lost the plot and began to push and shove their way around, desperately grabbing for some hold on reality, no matter how tenuous. Human flesh, living, breathing people offered them that grounding point. Taking control and dominating was the next level. Pushing people down rose the dominant above the weak. It established an order, in the mind at least, and there, in the chaos, people found their peace.

With the deck well sealed, and their numbers as large as they were, Eric understood that they had a chance to survive. To hold their ground and wait for the rescue that would surely come when it was noticed the ship was in distress.

"If only we could call the Justice League," Eric joked at Tara, whose hand seemed to have locked around his, her grip incapable of being broken.

"What?" she asked, clearly not getting the reference.

"Sorry, comic book humour. My full geek comes out when I am stressed." Eric offered another smile, and was pleased when Tara returned one.

"I get it, but wouldn't the Avengers be better?" Tara looked at him.

"Marvel is never better," Eric replied.

"You are so cute." She laughed.

"Well, if we can't call them, then we will have to improvise," Eric said, tightening his grip on Tara's hand. He broke into a run, leaping the barricade that led to the small sun deck. Three bodies lay on the loungers, their wounds long since dry, and their heads nowhere to be seen.

Eric ignored them, tipping one of the sun loungers over, spilling the body to the floor. He climbed onto the now empty piece of deck furniture and stood looking over the deck.

"Everybody...everybody stop. Listen to me. You need to stop. We can be safe here." Eric called, but nobody listened.

"What are you doing?" Tara asked nervously.

"I'm doing what needs to be done," Eric answered her. "Listen to me, we need to calm down. We stand a better chance as a group than we do individuals. These things are tough, but we are tougher."

Eric bellowed his monologue until this throat was sore and his voice scratchy. By the time he finished, Eric had gone through his entire repertoire of motivational lines and memorized texts from the comics and movies he so loved.

By the time he was done, a group of people had formed, their eyes cast upward toward him. They, in turn, grabbed people, stopping them as they ran. From above the Lido deck, Eric watched as the word spread and one by one, people turned to face him.

It was then that the full weight of his actions filtered through to his brain. The people now looked to him for guidance. He had positioned himself as their leader, and that meant he appointed himself as the one making all the decisions.

"I'm not too sure what I am supposed to do now," he spoke under his breath to Tara, who stood beside him.

She took his hand and leaned over to kiss his cheek. "Now you get to save them," she whispered.

Eric took a moment to focus himself. This cruise was not going the way he had planned.

"Listen to me, this ship is overrun, sure, but it is not lost. We are not far from land. The captain is still in control of the ship. He will bring us to safety. We just need to stay strong. If we stay together, as a unit, then we will survive this. Look around. Everybody is scared, but together we managed to block this place off well enough to keep the dead at bay. Imagine what we can do if we keep calm and work as a team." Eric could see that people were listening to him. He felt the weight of their collective gaze, but it did not slow him down. He fed off it.

"We can't just hide here. My wife is inside. I just came out for a smoke," a voice replied from the masses.

This instantly set off a series of murmurs, and the group began to disperse, their integrity only as strong as the weakest in the group.

"I understand, but alone you don't stand much of a chance. We have two choices. We can sit here, together, and wait for help to come, or we can split into groups. Men, women and children, or something like that. No, that won't work. I want everybody with any form of combat experience to group together on the left. That's military, police, boxing, anything that shows us you could fight. Then I want families together over on the right." Eric watched as the mass separated, and people moved from one side to the other. Many people appeared indecisive, flitting from left to right. Eric didn't want them, and made a note of as many as he could. If they chose the left, he would find a way to move them.

The groups formed, with the majority of people choosing the right-hand side. He didn't blame them.

Something growled at Eric's feet. He looked down and saw a severed head. The jaw snapped at air, while below the stump of neck, slithers of flesh danced around an extending section of neck and spine.

Eric bent down and pulled the head up, holding it aloft by the hair, a modern day Jason displaying the head of Medusa.

"These creatures can be killed and we can be saved. I want everybody in the left-hand group to prepare; we are going to start fighting back now. I want you to split into two groups. Each group will move in a different direction though the decks. Anybody we find, we bring out here. We can save people on this ship, we can be the heroes," Eric called and without thinking, he cocked back his arm and launched the head over the deck, off the boat and into the ocean.

The act was greeted by a round of applause that seemed to further unite them all as a single group.

"Are you sure you know what you are doing?" Tara asked as Eric moved away from the edge to head down to the Lido deck.

"I have no idea, but I can't let these people spend their time here in fear. Alone, those things will pick us off. At least now they have a chance." Eric smiled.

Tara leaned in and kissed him.

CHAPTER 20

Derrick woke as if rising from a bad dream. He looked around the room. His eyes took in the carnage, the utter devastation, before his mind could process what had happened.

"Celia, Michael...Carol?" he called out, jumping to his feet.

The room looked foreign, and nothing felt real, as if he was still dreaming, wading through en-route to the real moment of wakefulness

Derrick turned and saw his wife's body on the floor. Everything came flooding back to him. He saw the corpse, the second life beaten out of it with the aid of a tired-looking iron.

Derrick sank back to his knees on the floor and began to sob.

"I hated you," he growled, a flash of anger charging through him. "If you didn't run around fucking every man that came your way, we would not have been on this boat."

The anger swelled up inside him, stemming the tears, giving way to a rage the strength of which terrified him.

Derrick walked over to the mini bar and pulled every bottle free. He closed it and waited. The delivery system was still active.

"Thank fuck something works around here," he scoffed, tearing the lid off three different bottles and drinking the contents all at once. He threw the empties at his wife's corpse. "You ruined my life. I loved you and you fucking ruined my life. I guess we will never know how many people you fucked behind my back." The tears came again, but tears of anger; they burned his cheeks with their raging heat.

Derrick opened the remaining bottles and downed them one by one. "If I'm going to be stuck on this boat, I may as well get loaded, right?" He laughed and fell onto the bed.

The sudden rush of alcohol hit him hard. The ball of warmth in his gut sat and simmered slowly. The initial burn died down, leaving him feeling confrontational.

He opened the fridge and pulled another handful of bottles free. He drank them steadily, opening one, draining it and waiting, giving the heat time to spread. Hoping it could gnaw away at the numbing pain that was slowly stripping him to the bone.

"Why did you do it?" he asked his wife.

Because I was scared.

The answer came from nowhere, whispered on the air. Derrick sat upright, and looked around. The room was spinning, but he was on his own.

I was scared, baby. I never meant for it to get that out of hand.

"Then why? What was there to be scared of? Was our life that bad? We built up a good life, a family. I never treated you bad, never." Derrick was yelling now. "Why did you break my heart?"

I didn't want to get old. I needed to feel young again. Don't you remember what it was like when we were young? The feel of skin on skin, the electric rush of our bodies coming together?

"Excuses, that's all they are. You are giving yourself excuses, anything to help you sleep at night. You don't go around fucking half the town just because you're getting older. I was there, every night. I loved you, every night. Why couldn't you love me?" Derrick felt the rage subside, and so knocked back another miniature bottle of spirit. It only seemed to increase the ache he felt. As if he were being pulled in two.

I did love you. Until the very end, I loved you.

"Lying bitch!" Derrick roared, throwing the empty bottles of drink across the room. One hit and shattered the mirror that hung on the wall. Glass shards fell everywhere, surrounding Carol's body.

Derrick walked over to her, stumbling on booze-filled legs. He looked down at his wife, and saw her face staring back at him. Her mashed and mangled face repeated a hundred times over in the fragments of mirror that lay over the floor.

Her eyes stared at him, covering him from all angles so that there was no possible escape for him. The weight of their collective gaze was too much for him.

"I'm sorry. I loved you, I loved you and I want you back. Take me back...take me back." Derrick collapsed to his knees and pulled his wife toward him, cradling her broken head in his arms, smoothing her blood-and-brain-encrusted hair as tired tears blurred his vision.

CHAPTER 21

Captain Rasheed and his men led Jeff and Nour through the boat and down to the security area. Once there, they buzzed in and shoved the two men into one of the holding cells. The doors locked automatically. They were designed, not for maximum-security storage, but mainly to contain drunks or the occasional yob who was more interested in fighting than enjoying the ship's luxurious facilities.

"You two will not ruin this for us. The trial will go ahead, and this ship will be destroyed," Captain Rasheed growled at the pair.

"Why?" Jeff asked.

"This was just a test run. A trial. We needed to see how the pathogen would work in a closed environment. Controlled to a degree, but free to run rampant at the same time." The captain sneered, his sweaty skin glinting under the lights.

"You will not get away with this," Nour began.

"Silence, you fool. You think we don't know who you are. We have informants everywhere. We knew you were coming aboard this ship before you even received your orders," Rasheed snarled, revealing horribly yellowed teeth.

Nour stared the man down, and smiled.

"So what, you kill us all, sink the ship and what, release this plague on the world? What do you gain? Those things will eat you, too." Jeff's mind was reeling.

"That is because you are thinking too small. I am not surprised. You are a military man, small is what you are all about." Captain Rasheed cleared his throat, and spat a thick wad of yellow phlegm onto the floor. "These creatures are killing machines, my friend. Like all machines, they can be controlled. This is the first phase in a new era of warfare. We wanted to see what our creations could do when placed into a simulated general population. I must say, the results have been very impressive. The rate at which people are turning is good, and within the levels we accounted for. The next phase is to see how they do when only left with each other. Once we sink this ship and remove all trace of our presence here, we will begin phase two."

"You don't know how to control them yet, do you?" Jeff made the conclusion.

"Do not begin to guess what we can and cannot do, my friend." Captain Rasheed tried hard to hide the fact that Jeff was right.

"If you can't control them, what are you going to do if one of these things escapes the ship?" Jeff asked, his brain running through all manner of simulations.

"We are on a boat, my friend. We are in the middle of the ocean, and my men are watching for me to give the signal to sink this vessel. There is nowhere for them to go. People are scared, and hiding. Terror has always been a great way to control the masses, and this new physical form is the beginning of their re-education in fear." There was a gleam in Rasheed's eyes that sent a shudder running through Jeff like a cold winter wind. He was enjoying it all; he found joy in watching the dead rise, in being responsible for so much death.

"You will not get away with this. There are others watching your movements," Nour began, stepping forward to slap his hands against the door.

"What is important there, my friend, is that you are believing this. Your Interpol offices are a joke. You can run around pretending to be oh-seven, but really you are nothing." Rasheed spat again, this time against the window of the door.

The two men watched as the ball of snot snaked down the door like a slug, leaving a greasy trail behind as it went.

"It's double-oh-seven, and we knew what you were planning," Nour offered his response.

"You know what we allowed you to know. You don't understand. This has been planned for so long. It did not start with me, and it will not end with me. This is the future, not some pathetic attempt to instil fear. This is a quest for power and control. Do not forget that," Rasheed snarled and stormed away.

The two men stood in silence, looking around the cell.

It was a small, rectangular room with a bench running across the wide rear wall. Everything was new, meaning the cell had not yet taken on the lingering and unavoidable odour of drunkenness. One positive could at least be gleaned from their situation.

"Do you have any bright ideas, double-oh seven?" Jeff asked with a smile.

"I have a trick or two up my sleeves," Nour replied as he took off his watch.

"Really, spy gadgets in a watch?" Jeff asked, equal parts impressed and cynical of the cliché.

"No, I'm just putting it into my pocket so it doesn't get broken. This cost me a lot of money," he answered.

"Of course." Jeff could feel his cheeks redden.

"Besides, the explosives are in my cuff links," Nour added as he slid the links from his shirt sleeves and wedged them against the door, just above and below the locking mechanism.

"What?" Jeff stared, open-mouthed.

Nour said nothing, but waited patiently. A few moments later there, was a crackling sound, like a badly connected wire, and the door popped open.

Nour gathered his cufflinks and replaced them in his shirt sleeves before pushing open the door and walking out.

None of the men expected their emergence. The two men left to guard them were not even watching the monitors, but stood around a laptop, engrossed in a series of horse races playing out on a simulated racetrack.

Nour grabbed one, while Jeff took the other. They overpowered them, and shoved their unconscious forms into the cell, closing the door and blocking it with a desk.

"We need some weapons," Nour spoke as he turned around.

They could not access the central weapon store, which needed an authorized fingerprint in order to open the doors, but armed themselves with the pistols their guards carried.

Together they headed out into the third deck. "Where to?" Jeff asked, looking at Nour the way someone would regard a celebrity.

"The bridge. We need to alert the captain, and I need to make a phone call," Nour answered.

They rode the emergency lift up to the bridge, emerging to find the main bridge door open, and the sound of gunfire rattling from within.

The two men ran from the lift and found cover in the crew mess area. Jeff was aware that the door should have been closed, sealing in the dead from the bridge. He gave the order to move them before he left on his foolish endeavour.

"Move," Nour mouthed to Jeff, and the two men left the mess area, and hurried toward the bridge.

They only had one chance to surprise Rasheed and his men, which meant they needed to make their shots count.

Jeff watched Nour, and counted down, giving the signal for their entry.

They burst into the bridge, guns ready. Three men stood guard on the bridge, but Rasheed was not one of them. The first one went down before he even had the chance to turn around, catching a bullet in the neck. He collapsed, choking on his own blood, which leaked from him in thick dark red gulps.

The other two dropped to the floor behind one of the computer terminals, determined to make a last stand.

Nour motioned to Jeff, and he listened, reacting on instinct. He moved forward, ducking behind the nearest terminal. He moved gracefully, not making a sound as he rounded the bodies. Jeff squeezed off a round, firing toward the two men, buying Nour enough time to move forward.

The bridge was large, but when filled with bodies and four armed men, the space soon disappeared. It was a waiting game. One that Nour and Jeff won. They each moved down a different side from the main terminal, rounding the machines to face the two men.

"Give it up," Jeff snarled at them, kicking away the guns they dropped. "Get up."

The two men listened to the order, rising to their feet. Neither spoke, and neither made any attempt to move.

"What do you want to do with them?" Jeff turned to ask Nour.

It gave the men the only chance they needed. Lunging forward, one of them grabbed at Jeff, while the other pulled a knife from behind his back.

Nour fired two quick shots, which created two neat holes, one in the centre of each man's forehead. The knife clattered to the floor, and Jeff breathed a sigh of relief.

"Fuck, I've been out of the game far too long." He tried to laugh the incident off, but knew he did not sound convincing.

The two men looked around the bridge. The bodies of the remaining crew lay in pools of blood. Jeff gave a cry when he saw Joe's body. His throat had been cut, the deep slice moving from ear-to-ear, coming close to disappearing around his throat and onto his neck.

"I'm sorry, Joe," Jeff whispered to his long-time friend. He got to his feet and turned around.

He saw the four undead creatures ambling their way. They had ignored the entire firefight while they feasted on the freshly dead crew.

He recognized the men, Ibrahim, Issam, Zahi and Ahmad, nice guys, young and enthusiastic. Jeff liked them. Now, they had been reduced to snarling monsters, their bloodstained faces contorted by death and a second life nobody would wish for.

"What do we do?" Jeff asked Nour.

Nour backed up and pulled a pen from his pocket. Jeff drew a sharp breath. Nour looked over at him and smiled; he clicked the pen and heard Jeff take a sharp breath. He also heard the disappointed exhalation when he used the pen to write a note on a piece of blood-encrusted paper.

Jeff read the note, and nodded. They moved out of the room slowly, the four second-lifers closing on them. They skirted around them and out of the bridge, moving quickly back into the mess area.

"How do you know it is bugged in there?" Jeff asked, keeping his voice to a whisper.

"They know too much. You heard them. They have eyes everywhere, my friend," Nour answered as he leaned against the mess hall door with all of his weight. The four undead men on the other side continued to hammer against the door.

"How long until your back-up arrives?" Jeff asked, adding his own weight to the door.

"Not soon enough. They have seen what these things can do. They did not come up here just to kill the captain. They came here to signal the clean-up crew. They will kill everybody on this ship and then sink it." Nour still wore the cool, calm expression of a man doing nothing more out of the ordinary than taking his dog for a stroll.

"How do you know? You knew something was going to happen on this cruise, didn't you?" Jeff's voice became accusatory.

"We have been following this group for some time. They are smart and they are dangerous. We received information that told us something was going to happen, but this is not anything we ever considered. Reanimating the dead, that is the stuff of nonsense." Nour was almost apologizing with his answer.

"Not anymore," Jeff answered. "We need to stop that clean-up crew from getting on board. There are still people on this ship, people who can be saved."

The crashing against the door ceased, and for a moment the pair thought that it was already too late.

"It is still dark; we could get people into lifeboats," Nour offered.

"We need to get people off the ship. It's the best option I've heard. How do we get people to listen to us, and keep them away from those terrorists?" Jeff stared at Nour, and could tell he had an idea.

"I will sound the alarm, put out a distress call. You need to go find Rasheed; he needs to be stopped at all costs." Nour's expression changed now, and Jeff understood what he was saying.

"He is the one in charge, isn't he? Not just on this ship, but of this whole terrorist cell." Jeff didn't need to hear Nour's answer.

"Let's do this. Sound the alarm and head down to the security deck. That's where Rasheed will be. I'm sure of it. Meet me down there and then we will figure out what to do with this clean-up crew."

"What about the passengers?" Nour asked.

"People will always fight back when threatened." Jeff knew he could not save everybody.

"No, I mean, if I make the call, even my employers will not allow people to leave this ship." Nour's face was grave.

"You mean to tell me Interpol will just have us killed?" Jeff scoffed at the notion.

"Interpol, no, but I work for an agency many levels above what you know. They will sink this ship to keep the virus from spreading. I...I don't want innocent blood on my hands." The emotion was now flowing through Nour's facial expressions.

"Leave it with me, I have an idea," Jeff replied, thinking back to the man he had seen trying to stop the jumpers on the Lido deck. "Just sound the alarm, and come find me."

The two men shook hands, and paused.

"Thank you, my friend. Be quick, these people will sink the boat and kill us all without any hesitation," Nour said as they pushed the door open and ran back out onto the bridge deck.

CHAPTER 22

Robert moved through the ship, cutting a swathe of destruction in his wake. While making his way down the stairs, he had acquired a fire axe. He allowed himself the luxury to declare the emergency required in order to break the glass.

With the sharp, heavy weapon in his hands, he felt much stronger. He moved down the stairs quickly, making it as far as the seventh deck before a thick crowd of second-lifers filled the stairwell. They turned toward him, but their broken and mangled bodies were tied up in a mash of shattered limbs. Death saw them fall down the stairs, piling upon one another, until they became a single intertwined unit of leaking body fluids and sore wounds.

Exiting onto deck seven, Robert found himself face-to-face with a gaggle of the undead. They turned to him, as if caught unawares of by his presence.

Their hunched, hungry forms spun to attack, but Robert was quicker. He raised his axe and gave a roar as he moved in for the kill.

The blade cut through the air with a song-like swoosh, cleaving heads from shoulders. Gouts of black blood shot into the air, tainting it with the sour-smelling stench of rot. Robert swung and swung, dropping first five, then ten, fifteen, maybe even twenty bodies, littering the floor of the deck with them in various stages of disassembly. When Robert stopped, he was exhausted; panting, sweating, and covered from head to toe in blood, he leaned on the axe and looked around. Satisfied, he considered it to be a good job jobbed, and moved forward. The seventh deck was crowded with death. Bodies lay everywhere, several still alive, gargling and reaching for him, stretching as if this wandering stranger was the reaper coming to claim then, the slightest of touches from his axe being enough to claim their souls, and put them at peace.

Robert accepted that the second-lifers were dead. They shared nothing with the people they had been. Armed with that knowledge, killing them became that much simpler for him. The living posed a different problem. While he knew he could not save them, and he knew the fate that awaited them, Robert could not bring himself to end their suffering.

Robert wept as he wandered the deck, taking in the full extent of the death toll revealed to him.

He reached a restaurant, Big Shaq, a barbeque place. Thick black smoke wafted out from the kitchen, carrying with it the retch-worthy stench of burned meat. The last thing the boat needed was a fire, especially one that was out of control.

The floor that led to the kitchen was slick with blood, which, after a while, turned into a sickly sweet, sticky pool. It was only as he stood by the door into the kitchen area that Robert realized that the blood became barbeque sauce just before the door. It was leaking from a large, overturned vat beneath the counter.

Opening the door, the stench in the kitchen only grew worse. It was not hard to pinpoint the cause.

The dead left a trail of destruction wherever they went. Only, it appeared that the chefs refused to go down without a fight. Four bodies littered the floor, faceless cadavers, reduced to nothing more than meat sacks. One of the undead still stood in the kitchen, pinned to the worktop by two large chef's knives. They penetrated through each shoulder, lodging into the surface beneath. The creature flopped and floundered around as the hot stove it had been pinned to cook the meat off its face.

Robert approached slowly, and the creature sensed hm. It craned its neck upward, staring at the fresh delivery, the pain and torment of the stove now forgotten. The flesh of its face bubbled and dripped from the skull like melted plastic. The lips, which were all but fused together, thick strings of skin connecting upper and lower lips, oozed like fresh cheese on a piping hot pizza as the creature snapped and snarled in Robert's direction.

One of the dead man's eyes had exploded, cooking against the thing's skin like an egg white.

"Jesus wept," Robert said as he raised up the axe and put the creature out of its misery.

Pulling both of the knives free, understanding that having enough weapons was a necessity, Robert left the kitchen and the lingering odour of charred flesh.

He dispatched three more second-lifers on his way through the deck. By the time he reached the casino, another seven bodies were added to his total.

The casino was a large, cordoned-off area of the deck, consuming just over a third of the total space. The area was split into two sections. A general area, filled with slot machines and general low-level gambling options, and a dressier area. A place filled with tables and croupiers in smart clothes and free drinks.

Robert moved through the casino, looking around for anything he could find that would either help his survival or give him another target to kill.

The gambling machines and general area was a mess. Machines had been tipped over, used as weapons to crush the dead. It worked in some instances. The creatures moved too slow and showed no sign of instant reaction to danger. One on one, they were not too big of a threat, provided you kept your cool. Only once they formed a group did they become truly dangerous to anybody willing to fight back.

Coins littered the floor like lost treasure, spilled from the bellies of the beasts as they fell. A crash from the rear area of the casino got Robert moving. He held the axe in two hands, raised up against his right shoulder, ready to use when the time came.

He could see three second-lifers stumbling around back by the real gambling tables. They moved as a unit, individuals drawn by a common goal. That told Robert that there were people back there, hidden among the craps and Blackjack tables.

Robert moved quickly, his focus on the dead. The living had the choice, run, fight, or die. The axe swung down and split the first creature's head all the way down to the neck. The two halves of skull flopped to either side, the cheeks resting on the shoulders. The body fell inward on itself, pulling itself free of the blade as it fell.

Robert saw the living. Two people huddled together, doing their best to defend themselves with a couple of lumps of blood-stained wood. They chose to fight. Robert liked them.

Turning, he slapped with the axe, smacking the broad side rather than the edge of the blade, into the face of the second, before twisting the axe in his hands and swinging to the other side, burying the blade in the soft, blubbery gut of the third creature. A large man with long hair and a poor attempt at a beard, the obese second-lifer doubled over, more from the force of the blow than any recognition of pain. Robert grabbed one of the knives from his belt and stabbed down through the back of the man's skull.

The three second-lifers were dead, for good this time. Something was still moving; Robert could hear it ticking. He turned around, the knife still clutched in his hand. The roulette wheel was turning, knocked into action by the force of the slapped dead man's fall. One of the eyeballs, knocked free by the forceful slap delivered by the axe, sat in black thirteen.

Robert turned to look at the two people. The couple stared at him with wide-eyed wonder.

"You saved us," the woman spoke. She was very attractive, and had a distinctive accent.

"Don't mention it. You need to get out of here," Robert answered, turning to walk away.

"You need to come with us," the man answered. From his chiselled good looks, it was easy to picture them as a couple.

"No, thank you. I can't just walk away. These things are everywhere," Robert answered.

"Then we are coming with you," the girl snapped back instantly.

"Like hell you are," Robert said, turning around in shock at the audacity of their offer.

His words carried through the empty casino.

"My name is Sofia. This is Jose. We are here on our honeymoon, and now we are going to help you. I don't know what is happening, but people are dying. My daddy didn't raise me to sit back and watch people suffer." Sofia crossed her arms over her chest and stood with a pout on her lips.

"You won't win," Jose added after a while, with Robert and Sofia engaged in a staring contest.

"Fine," Robert said, resigned.

They moved out onto the deck, back past the barbeque restaurant and the lounge.

"Why are you doing this?" Robert asked as he swung his axe, decapitating a second-lifer that wandered out of the lounge area to their left.

"I told you, my daddy didn't raise me like that," Sofia answered.

"I bet he doesn't want you to go kill yourself, either," Robert replied, confused as to why the young couple seemed so eager to help.

"I can take care of myself," Sofia quipped, and as if to prove her point, she threw her leg out in a kick that saw her hips swivel, her leg extended vertically against her body and then down, heel first, into the face of a dead woman that was heading their way. She followed it up with two jabs with the knife she took from Robert.

"I can see that." Robert was impressed. "But still, I'm not doing this to be a hero. You don't want to be around me." He wanted to push them away.

"Well, we're not either, but I won't sit back and watch people die. So you are stuck with us," Sofia answered. "Isn't that right, honey?"

Jose smiled and winked at Robert. "Yep, you're stuck with us." He smiled again and leaned over to kiss his wife.

Robert grunted and turned away.

"So, what's your story?" Jose asked as they made their way up the stairs to the next deck. He eyed up the twisted mass of second-lifers that blocked the stairwell to the lower decks. Their hungry growls made him misstep and stumble.

"Not much to tell," Robert said, pushing open the door to the eighth deck.

"Everybody's got a story," Sofia said, her voice cheerful in spite of everything.

"My story is one you don't want to hear." Robert stopped and turned to look at them.

"Maybe, but what if we are the last ones you can ever tell it to?" She looked at him, her eyes drawing him in, weakening him. She really was beautiful.

"My wife left me a few months ago." Robert threw the words at them.

"Why?" Sofia pushed, knowing there was more to tell.

"Drop it," Robert snapped, his voice going deep, a growl behind his words.

Sofia stopped, both talking and walking. She let Robert build a head start on them, keeping Jose by her side.

"What's his problem?" Jose asked, his dislike for Robert beginning to grow.

"He's broken. Something broke him before he came here," Sofia answered, watching Robert move. He swung the axe and cut through a second-lifer that emerged from within one of the cabins.

"Great, so we picked up a pet." Jose smiled and kissed his wife's head. Sofia was a caring person, and when she set her sights on someone, she would ensure she helped them in whatever way she could. It was one of the things he loved the most about her, but at the same time, one of her most infuriating qualities.

"I can help him," Sofia said, moving off after Robert, who busied himself by dispatching a family of the undead that appeared from one of the rooms ahead of them.

The eighth deck was only cabins, and with many of the doors closed and locked, they made short work of the deck. They wasted no time in checking each room. Robert moved at his own pace, never stopping to look for Sofia or Jose, never once asking them to take the lead or check something.

He was relentless, he was ruthless, and he was a wreck. Tears streamed down his face as he swung, each blow more than just death to one of the undead, but an attack on death itself, the son of a bitch who seemed so intent on destroying his life.

CHAPTER 23

Eric moved from the sun deck down to the main area, stepping around the splattered bodies of the dead.

As he expected, the group divide slanted heavily toward those unskilled for the task at hand. Not many people had the skills required to fight back against the undead. He was fully aware that there were some who should be in the smaller group, but who chose the safer option. He understood their decision.

He looked around, feeling the weight of the gazes upon him. He felt a rush of nerves, but they fell away the moment he opened his mouth to speak.

"Nobody here—" Eric began, but the sound of rotor blades beating in the night sky cut his words short.

Everybody turned their gaze to the sky. The sound was unmistakable, yet there was nothing to be seen but an endless sea of stars.

Nobody cheered or made much sound at all. They all remembered what had happened to the last chopper that visited the ship.

"I don't see anything," someone finally spoke, and soon whisperings spread like wildfire.

They turned to screams the moment the guns started to fire.

Bullets tore through the air, punching through flesh and bone, living and dead alike. A stream of hot lead rained down on them from the darkness. Sparks flew as bullets ricocheted off the ship's railings and walls.

Glass shattered under the barrage of fire, and above all else, people screamed.

Beside him, Eric saw a young woman take a shot through the face. One minute she stood beside him, the next her face blossomed outward like a raw meat flower. Eric could have sworn she even managed to turn around and look at him before she collapsed.

A coating of warm blood covered Eric's face as another passenger took a round to the throat, tearing their carotid artery to pieces.

Eric turned and pulled Tara to the floor. "Get down," he screamed.

Lying face-first on the floor, his hands over his head, Eric tasted blood. Not his, but the blood of those cut down. He gagged but didn't move. He still had no idea where the attacking helicopter came from, and he did not want to risk being killed himself to find out.

The screaming echo of gunfire stopped, and the chopper turned away. Eric looked around from the floor. The ship had been decimated. The wooden deck was smashed and broken glass lay everywhere after the strafing wave of fire had blown out every window.

All around them, people lay screaming. Eric soon learned that most people had not been killed outright by the attack. They had been shot, and their death was inevitable, for nobody would be there in time to save any of them. Their deaths would be slow, painful, and agonizing, both to them, and to the ears of those damned to survive.

Eric pulled himself to his feet, his heart thundering in chest. His head spun, and his gut churned like a raging sea. He bent over, resting on his knees and counted backward from ten. Over and over he counted, until his stomach settled. He looked down at his feet and saw a severed hand lying palm down. It looked as if it was giving him the finger.

"We need to get inside," he spoke, turning to take Tara and escape.

"All of these people. Who…who could do that?" She wept.

"We can't help them," Eric spoke hurriedly as a hand grabbed his ankle. An elderly man had clawed his way over to the pair, his body a bloody mass of skin and bone, his thin skin torn apart by the barrage. "I'm sorry."

Eric took Tara by the hand. He heard the sound of the approaching helo as it made its way around the ship for a second sweep.

"Run!" Eric yelled to anybody that would listen.

Gunfire came again, a single, constant stream that moved along the deck, cutting down the survivors as they ran.

Eric felt Tara pull him back, but he kept running, making sure their grip on each other was not broken. If they wanted to survive, they needed to get off the deck, to get away from the aerial assault that rained down on them. He dove through the shattered remains of a window. Glass tore at his flesh as he fell to the floor, but he gritted his teeth and pulled himself through and into the relative safety of the inner deck.

Others shared the same idea, and as the helicopter pulled away again, a small group of survivors sought some meagre degree of satisfaction in the knowledge that they had survived. When they heard the helicopter making a second run, the majority of them huddled together and wept.

Eleven people survived the attack, including Eric and Tara. Out of them, one man was seriously wounded. He had taken a round through the back. The hole was the size of a fist, and everybody understood it was only a matter of time before he died. Three others had been shot, but their injuries did not appear to be severe enough to cause any great or pressing concern.

In the distance, the sun was starting to rise, the sky lightening in shade as the world readied itself for a new day. Eric saw it and realized, in all likelihood, they would never see it dawn.

"All of those people...will they...will they turn into those...things?" a scared young voice asked.

This set off another round of murmurs and overlapping discussion.

"I don't think it matters," Eric spoke up, the crowd silencing to let him speak.

"What do you mean?" the same scared voice asked. Eric looked, but he could not identify who spoke; the group was crowded too close together for any individual to be picked out.

Eric had no doubt, however, that the words formed a statement echoed by the collective.

"Because I don't think they will let us live until morning." Eric knew the time for lies and for rousing speeches was done. "I don't know who they are, but they opened fire on a deck full of innocent people, survivors. I think that is enough to tell us their intentions are not to act as our white knights."

"They are going to kill us all." Fear began to spread.

"They don't want the dead to leave this ship, and the best way to contain it is to simply get rid of it." Eric looked at the group, and they looked at him. He saw it in their eyes that they were expecting him to offer them the solution.

"Get rid of the ship, and get rid of us," a new voice from within the group expanded the sentence, capturing the very words Eric tried so hard to avoid.

The sound of the helicopter had faded into the background, but it was a constant presence. Someone broke away from the group and moved across the deck, peering out into the darkness.

"I see it. It's landing," the voice called out.

The inner portion of the Lido deck was a large open plain bar area, broken into three main service areas, with seating moving in all directions. A door sat at either end, one that gave way to the main hall area and the elevators, and the other moved towards a small open air, reservations only cocktail bar.

As if on cue, or serving as a timely reminder that their new unseen attackers were not the only problem with the ship, both doors opened and a horde of second-lifers flowed inside. They stumbled and tripped, somehow remaining upright. The general wafting odour of their decay flowed ahead of them, closely followed by their hungry growls.

"We need to fight back." Eric called.

"How--?"

"I don't want to die—"

"They are coming through the doors, too," voices cried out in panic, words overflowing words. Thoughts overriding action.

Eric saw that the barricade that had been set up along the long side of the deck had been decimated in the attack, allowing a fresh wave of death easy access to the entire deck.

"Quickly, outside," Eric ordered. "Grab anything you can to defend yourself with."

The dead came for them before they could so much as breathe, converging on all sides. Eric picked up a broken lump of wood and sprinted from one of the tables in the bar. He swung it like a baseball bat, decapitating the shambling, longhaired, bikini-clad figure that was closest to him.

He turned to grab Tara but she was not behind him. Not directly at least. She was fighting off an undead man whose groping hands craved contact with her flesh.

Eric swung his lump of wood, bringing it crashing down across the dead shoulders. The second-lifer fell forward just as Tara stepped to one side and stabbed upward with a broken bottle. The glass lodged into the dead man's face, tearing deep gouges into the flesh.

"Come on," Eric spoke.

Tara reached for him and flinched. Eric saw the blood spreading down her side. He froze, all the fight draining from him.

"I got shot, not bit. Let's get out of here while we still can." Tara strode forward, walking into Eric's hand rather than reaching for it.

The dead moved like a flood. They showed only minimal interest in the lead-tainted meat that lay strewn over the deck. While several fell face-first into the bounty of death, most kept moving, drawn by the sounds of fear and the scent of terror-infused flesh.

"We can't get out," Tara cried as the rest of their group fell to the dead. Eric turned away as their relentless rage saw a man ripped in half, pulled so fiercely in each direction that his navel tore open and spilled his guts straight into the hungry mouths of those that had fallen to the floor in feast.

"We have to try, this way. I have an idea." Eric sprang to life, moving across the deck with purpose.

They dodged around a trio of the undead, who made a half-hearted attempt to grab them, but fell into the category of second-lifers that were happy to feast on the bullet-riddled dead.

To their left, a figure came running, screaming and shouting, waving a thick shard of glass in the air. The man's hand had been torn to shreds by the sharp shard. From the state of the severed neck that extended from the head clamped onto his crotch, it was clear to understand why he was so frantic. The fleeing figure stared at Eric as he ran by. Blood bubbled from his lips, but before he could make any sound other than an expression of pain, he disappeared. The man fell into the swimming pool and disappeared into a churning pool of red.

He splashed and thrashed around on the surface as the water bubbled up around him, pink froth forming on the surface. The pool was filled with death, the drowned figures moving like piranhas, attacking any intruder into their domain.

"There are too many, we can't go through them," Tara gasped, her free hand now clamped against her side.

"Then we go over them. This way." Eric found the energy to raise a smile before helping Tara up the ladder.

They climbed high above the deck, leaving the crowd behind them. The second-lifers showed no inclination to follow them.

They reached the upper platform and suddenly the size of the ship came into focus. The gentle wind reminded them that the boat was at sea, a fact easily forgotten both before and after the dead rose. Yet, as they stood on the platform, high above the carnage, the feeling of being trapped and isolated was never stronger.

"What do you have in mind?" Tara asked.

"We need to get away from this herd. That helicopter could not mean anything good. We need to get to a lifeboat and get off this ship before it really is too late." Eric picked up the equipment at their feet and strapped them both in while he talked.

"I don't think I can do this." Tara stuttered, looking more terrified in that moment than at any other point in time.

"Just hold on to me," Eric said.

Tara moved into his arms and kissed him on the cheek. "Just for good luck," she smiled. "That's what they said in Star Trek right?"

"Star Wars, I think. I've never seen it," Eric answered.

"What?" Tara gasped.

"Hey, not all geeks like Star Wars. I'm more of a Flash kind of guy. Are you ready?" Eric didn't wait for an answer. In the distance, across the boat, the sound of gunfire punctured the early morning air.

The rig was not designed to support two people in an embrace, and as they jumped, they came apart.

The zip line ran along the boat, taking them over the pool and the rest of the Lido deck, over the main inner section and down to the rear portion, moving on a gentle diagonal.

Tara screamed as they whizzed through the air, the line screeching as if it was in pain as they sped along.

"Hold on," Eric called to her, shouting against the wind they created.

Beneath them, the dead paid them no mind, but the haunting gaze of the dying cut Eric to the quick.

They reached the other side of the zip line area, and Eric reached out to grab hold of the railings. There was nobody standing there ready to catch them. They had to do everything alone.

Pulling themselves onto the platform, Eric shimmied out of the harness and turned to help Tara. She stared at him with hazy eyes. Her face was white, and blood streamed from her wound.

"Tara," Eric began, but before he could grab her, she fell. Still attached to the harness and the zip line, Tara floated in mid-air. Eric knew she was dead. She never moved, never cried out, she just hung still. An overwhelming sense of grief flooded over him. A sensation that seemed out of place for the loss of someone he had known less than twenty-four hours.

Beneath him, the rattle of gunfire continued, closer now. Eric needed to leave. He took one last look at Tara, hoping for a miracle. He willed her to move, to wake up. She did not. She merely hung in the air, suspended like a piece of meat in a butcher's back room.

Back on the deck, Eric searched for the respite he so desperately gambled on finding. There should have been a lifeboat on the rear portion of the deck. Everything was there, the station, the pulley and the ropes that held the covers in place. Everything apart from the life raft.

The initial growl startled him, but Eric spun around and came face-to-face with a rather bloodied dead man, whose face had been peeled backward, the skin rolled up onto his forehead where it sat like a roller blind, ready to be drawn when some perception of reality was required.

Eric moved around the creature, and slid back inside. More of the dead waited for him. A group of survivors battled against the unending presence of the second-lifers.

Bravely they battled against a group of the undead, but slowly they fell to the horde. The living grew tired as they fought, while the dead just kept going, relentless.

Several turned to face Eric, pulling away from the group to come after him. Eric had no weapons, and there was little he could do once he felt the wall against his back.

The first creature grabbed at him, and Eric moved to one side, punching the beast in the side of the head. Grimacing as his fist began to throb from the impact, Eric turned and kicked out at his second attacker. His foot connected with the dead man's knee, and the creature hit the floor, the ligaments in its join snapping with a crisp, audible pop.

Eric turned his body and ran, squeezing through the gap between the two dead men, and right into the arms of a third.

Cold, powerful arms closed around him in a hug. Pain tore through his body as teeth clamped down on his shoulder. The second-lifer's head wrenched as he tore the flesh free, chewing it noisily in Eric's ear.

The pain was all-encompassing. It blocked out almost everything. The only thing Eric clung on to was his will to live. He kicked and thrashed and managed to break free from the grip.

He pushed himself away, his left arm on fire. He turned and more stood waiting for him.

He dodged the attack when once again, teeth clamped down into his flesh. The dead man, whose knee Eric had broken, was there, its jaw closed around Eric's calf. Eric kicked and fought as he felt the teeth pierce his skin.

His vision blurred as meat and muscle tore free from his frame. Collapsing onto his knees, Eric roared in agony as the pack descended on him. His back tore open and he felt their cold, dead fingers hook into his flesh. Eric coughed and spat a stream of blood as he heard his spine snap under the weight of their grip.

Eric opened his mouth to scream, but a cold, dead hand punched into his throat and through to the back of his head.

CHAPTER 24

Derrick cradled his wife until her body was cold and the leaking fluids nothing but cool jelly on his skin.

He felt nothing. His whole body was numb. His brain was running, the wheels spinning, but he had left the track a long way behind him.

He replayed the final months of his life over and over, trying desperately to change things, to pinpoint the exact moment everything fell apart. To re-write history and give himself the ending that his family deserved.

He ran through every time he had caught his wife acting nervous or suspicious, the number of times she went out with a friend he had never met. If only he had stood up and challenged her, questioned where she was going. Maybe it would have been different.

He blamed himself because his wife had been in pain, and he had not noticed. He was too selfish, thinking more about what he was missing out on in life to stop and think about her needs.

Derrick remembered when Carol finally broke down and started her confession. He allowed himself to be consumed by a rage that came close to destroying him. He wanted to be rid of her, to go on living life with just his kids.

Kids…his mind threw their final moments at him. Michael's scream as the undead tore him apart. How his Celia had gotten sick. If only they had never come on the cruise, if only he had forgiven his wife, then they would not have come. If only he had loved her as much as she deserved, then she would not have cheated. They would still be together. It was all his fault. He had killed them.

Derrick laid his wife down and kissed her forehead one final time. He stood up, his body aching. His head throbbed and his mouth felt as if it had a fur lining.

He grabbed another bottle from the mini-bar and downed the contents. His head cleared a little and his mouth no longer tasted like a pub floor.

Outside his door, he heard them pacing. The dead. They knew he was in there. They knew what he had done; there could be no secrets from the dead. In his drunken state, Derrick understood why they came. The dead rose to make sure he got his just desserts.

"Forgive me," Derrick begged as he stepped over his wife and grabbed the door. He unlocked it, half expecting the dead to enter the room in a flood, but they didn't. There was nothing. Opening the door fully, he looked out into the hall. The corridor was empty, or rather, was empty of living or undead things. Only the genuinely dead lined the floor, their blood painting the walls.

Derrick walked the hall, stepping over the dead where he could.

He knew the dead were there, waiting. He could hear them.

"Come and get me," he called out, slapping his hands against the walls, hoping the noise would attract them.

The growls grew loud, echoing in his ears. It was as if the boat itself came alive to consume him.

The first shadows flickered on the wall, ambling silhouettes of the walking death that approached him. Derrick exhaled. His body shook and he knew that his time was up.

He collapsed to his knees as the mob of blood-covered dead rounded the corner. Their growls grew to a fervour when they saw the free meal that was offering itself up to them. Derrick watched them approach. A man and a woman shared the lead. The man was dressed in a pair of torn pyjamas, his belly torn open and hollowed out. The frayed flaps of skin waved as he walked, as if beckoning Derrick to them. The woman wore nothing, and luckily seemed considerably younger than the man beside her. Large breasts swung low and heavy, although one hung considerably lower than the other, but that was because it was only attached on one side, meaning it had more room to hang, and a greater range of swing to its movements.

They fell on Derrick, the woman's heavy tits slapping him in the face as she smothered him.

He felt pain, burning and unbearable, as eager teeth and fingers tore through his skin. He smelled the scent of his own blood, sweat and piss, before hearing his flesh being chewed and swallowed in a rush.

A strange calm washed over him. He lay back and closed his eyes. He pictured his family, his wife and kids, forcing his mind to recall happier times. Yet the only thing he saw was them, them as they were now. Dead. Their bodies ravaged and shredded. Flesh hanging in strips, large, open and weeping gouges torn into their flanks. He saw maggots crawling over them, their bodies searching for a nice moist place to sleep. He heard buzzing, and opened his eyes. He was alone; the dead had disappeared, their meal was over. There was nothing left to enjoy.

Derrick tried to move, but he couldn't. Everything grew dim, slowly drawing ever darker. He heard the buzzing again, and a fly appeared, circling his body, waiting for him to pass so that it could finally lay the eggs that would spawn the next generation.

CHAPTER 25

Nour ran from the officer's mess and headed straight for the bridge. He hurdled the bodies of the dead and grabbed the radio. He knew the frequency to select for a private transmission. He also knew that his employers would already be setting the wheels in motion. After all, he planted the bugs on the bridge.

He knew exactly what his employers would do with the ship. Even if his orders had stated it was a drill, a test for reasons of protocol, a controlled experiment in the face of the new war on terror. Nour had never met Rasheed before, and was convinced the man had no idea who he was. Rasheed was nothing but a cutthroat, a mercenary hired to do one job. Ensure the test run was contained.

Nour felt sick to his stomach knowing that he had been so influential in the death of so many. He smiled as he opened up the general communication channel and signalled the mayday alert.

He could see the faces of those who presented him with the assignment. Him, the good soldier, always willing to do what was deemed necessary. Recent years had been the toughest of his whole career. The threat of terrorism brought with it a stigma he hated, and yet now, at the end of his days, he was just as big a part of the problem as he was the cure.

Terror ruled the ship. He had played his part well, and he hated having to lie to Jeff. A man who was fighting for the right thing, regardless of the rest.

"Mayday, Mayday, this is the *Ocean Princess*, we need urgent assistance. We have terrorists on board the vessel. They have taken control. I repeat, terrorists have taken control of the vessel." Nour set his message to repeat over the emergency transmission and turned around.

He heard the growls coming from behind him, and he accepted his fate.

It was fitting that the same four dead men that ended his life had also welcomed him on board. Issam, Zahi, Ibrahim and Ahmed—the four surrounded Nour like a pack. They closed in on him, and he offered no resistance when they tore into his flesh. He screamed...he screamed until his voice died in his throat, but it was his deserved fate, and he accepted it.

Jeff turned left the moment he exited the mess hall, and never looked back. He knew they were against the clock, and he was running out of ideas.

Jeff didn't hear the helicopter approach, but he heard the automatic fire from the mounted guns, and watched from the twelfth deck as the crowd was slaughtered.

Jeff threw his body to the floor, pressing himself flat as the helo sprayed the boat with burning lead. The glass shattered, showering Jeff with flesh splitting shards. They also took out the two second-lifers that managed to sneak up on him.

Sprinting along the deck, Jeff watched as the man that he had seen rallying the people appeared. Jeff called to him, but only succeeded in drawing even more attention to himself.

Jeff ran through the crew quarters and out onto the smoking deck. He was greeted by a half-naked member of the crew, and two tattoo-covered women in equal stages of undress. The three squatted together against the wall. Jeff was not sure who screamed loudest when he burst through.

"We are getting off this ship. Get down to the lifeboats," Jeff ordered as he climbed over the railing and scrambled down the side of the boat, jumping down onto the eleventh deck.

Eric sped over his head, and was gone by the time Jeff rounded the rear of the boat. He saw the man's female companion dangling above the deck. A group of second-lifers stood beneath her, their mouths open, trying to catch the drops of blood that fell from her lifeless body.

Jeff hurried as fast as he could, spurred on by the sound of gunfire from across the ship. He arrived just in time to see a large undead woman rip Eric's head from his body.

"Shit," Jeff couldn't help but shout. He regretted it immediately, as the group of walking corpses turned to approach him. Jeff backed up, knowing he couldn't backtrack, because he had skirted around a growing group of second-lifers as he followed Eric.

The group closed in on him, and Jeff saw his chance. He ran, shoulder barging one of the dead out of his way. He felt their hands grabbing at him, but he refused to stop. He broke free and burst into the hallway, and didn't stop running until he reached the stairwell.

Panting, he stood and roared, slapping his hand against the wall, again and again, until the meaty thwack of his skin on metal wall fell away to a tired slap. When he was done, his hand burned, but it served to focus his mind.

From below him, deeper in the stairwell, the growl of the undead echoed up to him.

"Fuck you, fucking fuckers," Jeff roared, springing to his feet, driven by rage. "Fuck the whole fucking lot of you."

That was when he heard the scream, and the rattle of gunfire, two things Jeff thought he left behind long ago, but now seemed to be a normal component of his life once more. The shattering glass and the sudden rushing sound of water was new. Joe ran down to the tenth deck, his mind only able to connect the water to the sea, and therefore by the time he arrived, he was convinced the boat was taking on water.

CHAPTER 26

Captain Rasheed was waiting for the chopper to set down. He heard their blast of fire on the deck, and did not bat an eyelid at the thought of the innocent lives being lost. He did not work for the people who hired him. They came to him because of his special skills when it came to dealing with people.

The deaths of the passengers did not belong on his conscience, but on that of those who hired him. Rasheed's conscience was clear, just as it always was.

"Welcome aboard the *Ocean Princess*," he said with a cackled laugh as the leader of the squad stepped from the chopper.

Each man in the group was already fully dressed and fully up to speed with the situation on board. They did not speak, for there was no need. They moved as one, sweeping through like a plague. They had worked together on clean-up operations across the globe, but in recent years, the majority of their work had been based in the Middle East and the surrounding area.

Once a squad of soldiers, they sold their souls to enter the black ops world. Now they moved under the cover of night, swooping in, cleaning house and then heading home.

Rasheed stood before them, the smile beaming on his sweaty face. The group's CO stared at him, watching him through the visor of his helmet. He raised his weapon and fired, planting a bullet in the centre of Rasheed's forehead. Blood and brain burst out the other side of his shattered skull.

The CO turned to his men. They numbered eight in all. He pointed to two and closed his fist. The others he held up three fingers and pointed down side of the ship. Everybody nodded.

The first group, two specially-trained individuals, grabbed a case from the back of the chopper and headed off. They made their way down to the lower level where they would place the explosive charges that would sink the ship and hide all traces of their presence. The remaining five men followed their CO, moving down one side of the ship, their assault rifles at the ready and a string of grenades shared between them for if things got truly dire.

The men moved in formation, cutting through the dead like a Roman phalanx. Their weapons dealt out death like justice. Heads and bodies exploded. Those not killed outright by the forward-facing bodies in the front of the formation met their maker courtesy of those in the rear.

A medium-sized group of survivors who chose to barricade themselves in the business rooms on the same deck opened the doors at the sound of gunfire, convinced their salvation had arrived. They met a stream of bullets that ripped them open and sent blood and guts spilling to the floor in a sea of death and destruction.

The group moved on, moving through the ship, floor by floor, room by room. The front and rear lines took out the general population while those on the flanks opened every door and took care of what they found. Never did they break formation other than to swap positions before they started each new deck. That was not a specific part of their strategy, but even when cleaning up and doing the necessary it was important to be fair and not have one person hog all the glory.

Deck by deck, floor by floor, they left destruction in their wake, all the way to the tenth floor, where even they found themselves pausing before the spectacle that was the on board aquarium.

CHAPTER 27

"Behind you," Sofia called out the warning as she slashed out with her chef's knife and split open the dead woman's throat.

The injury itself did not slow the second-lifer down any more than the eviscerating gash that rose vertically from her navel to just below her breasts. It did, however, give Sofia a better angle to force the knife through the woman's temple and into her brain.

Robert heard the warning and spun, decapitating two second-lifers with a single swing of his axe. Beside them, Jose was striking out with the knife in wild uncontrolled swings. It proved to be an effective tactic, albeit a tiring one.

The trio moved through the two lower levels without too much problem. They came across a few groups of the undead wandering the halls, but for the most part, the cabin doors were closed and locked. They could hear snarls and thuds coming from behind them, but they learned that so long as the dead were contained, the best practice was to move on.

They came across several survivors, but none seemed interested in taking up arms and joining the fight. The majority tuned and ran, heading for the outside, pleased to have been freed from the stifling confines of their room.

Now they were trapped. Stuck on the tenth deck, with the dead surrounding them, coming from either end of the corridor, while above and behind them sharks, turtles and all manner of fish and other ocean wildlife swam around, oblivious to the destruction being wrought around them.

The tenth deck of the ship was home to both the library and an enormous aquarium. The single, large display was set up like a tunnel, offering people the chance to walk under the sea. The tank proved to be a popular area for the living and dead alike. None of them knew whether the draw came from the water or because so many people gathered when the dead rose.

The trio found themselves pinned inside the tunnel; the dead crowded toward them, lined up five or six deep, each one eager to tear into their flesh.

"There are too many of them," Sofia cried as a large bearded man swung a clubbing blow in her direction.

Sofia ducked the blow and stabbed with the knife. The blade disappeared into the man's gut, and his body fell to the floor, pulling the knife from Sofia's hand as he fell.

There was no time for her to grab it back, because two more fell upon her. Hands closed around her arms, in vice-like grips. She screamed and heard the whoosh of air as the axe sliced through the arms, severing them just below the elbow, before changing direction to cleave the heads in half. One was sliced on a vertical axis, while the other was a blow that came horizontal, embedding itself ear-height into the skull.

Sofia screamed and backed up as the undead pressed closer against them. Robert ran out of room to swing the axe, and so started using it widthways to push back against the ranks of the undead.

Robert gave one final shove, roaring like a caged lion as he did. The axe was wrenched from his grip and the trio found themselves pushed to the floor by the weight of the mob.

The growls and grunts that surrounded them was deafening. They didn't even realize that the weight of the undead was lessening until it was too late. The automatic fire rolled like thunder in the mountains, tearing the undead apart. Globs of cold flesh peppered with hot lead fell all around them. One particularly feisty woman was perilously close to tearing a chunk from Sofia's neck when a bullet took out her jaw. Three teeth fell into Sofia's mouth, followed by the viscous black blood. Screaming, she shoved the dead woman from her and got to her feet.

They were dead, every last one of them. Their heroes stood at the far end of the underwater tunnel, five men dressed from head to toe in full military garb.

With their helmets, masks and thick full body armour, they looked like the main cast of a badass new sci-fi movie. They didn't move. They stared down at the trio, who stood side-by-side, returning the stares thrown their way.

"Thank you," Sofia spoke, her voice not much more than a broken squeak.

The central figure of the group flinched at her words, lifted his rifle ever so slightly and pulled the trigger.

Jose's head exploded in a puff of blood and bone. He collapsed to the floor as Sofia screamed. All five men raised the weapons, but Robert grabbed Sofia and pulled her to the floor. The burst of gunfire missed them both by inches, and instead burst through the aquarium wall. Water gushed from the dozen holes, the glass quickly splintering, radiating out from each entry point until the entire structure gave way.

"Run," Robert roared, pushing Sofia forward as the first sprouts of water hit his back.

He moved on instinct more than anything deliberate.

The walls of the aquarium exploded with a crushing blow that shook the entire deck. The force of the cascading water tore a larger and larger hole in the tank.

"Don't look back." Robert called, pushing Sofia in the back as she began to slow.

They leaped up the small flight of four stairs and leaned against the wall. Breathing hard, their energy spent, neither spoke, but both watched as a large shark thrashed on the floor, tearing apart one of the bodies of the second-time dead that floated its way.

"Who the hell was that?" Sofia asked in between deep gulps of air.

"I wish I knew," Robert answered, his words equally breathless.

"They killed Jose." Sofia stood with her back against the wall and slid to the floor. She sobbed with her head between her knees.

"Those guys are still out there. We need to move. We need to warn the other passengers." Robert rose to his feet and took Sofia by the hand.

He helped her to her feet and spun her around quickly as Jose's faceless form drifted into view from within the flooded tunnel.

"No, I won't leave him." Sofia began to thrash and kick, slapping out at Robert, who stood tall and let her hit him. None of this hurt more than the deep wound across his back he had picked up as they ran from the exploding glass tank.

"It's ok. It's going to be ok. We are going to get out of here." Robert offered the best form of consolation he could think of.

Sofia looked at him, her tears stemmed for the time being. A burst of gunfire rang out and refreshed the panic she had conquered.

Robert led the hyperventilating Sofia away from the aquarium. They could hear the heavy armour-clad footfalls of their newfound enemy echoing from the other side of the corridor.

They were trapped. Gunfire rang out in short, sharp busts. Effective, efficient and deadly. "Where are we going?" Sofia asked.

Before Robert could answer, a hand appeared out of the darkness, grabbing Sofia and covering her mouth. Robert moved to heave his axe but the muzzle of the gun aimed at his chest stemmed his anger.

"Shhh, keep quiet. I'm on your side. Come with me, now," Jeff whispered, not letting up on either his grip of Sofia or his aim on Robert.

"Who are you?" Robert asked,

"No time. Come on, I have a plan," Jeff whispered, and lowered the gun. "Don't scream."

Sofia nodded, aware that he was talking to her. Jeff removed his hand and disappeared into the darkness. He dipped through a small door that led into the aquarium's maintenance area.

A long narrow stretch that ran the length of the tank, it allowed them to move the other way, to the rear of the ship, effectively coming back around behind their attackers.

"We need to move fast. Up this way." Jeff led them to a ladder that rose above the tank.

Following without question, they climbed. Robert winced more with every rung he took. The blood felt cold against his fire-kissed skin, his strength failing him to such an extent that Jeff needed to pull him up the final rungs and into the comparative safety of the eleventh deck.

"Come on, buddy. I'm going to need your help with his," Jeff said to Robert as he helped him to his feet. "Everybody is counting on us."

Robert heard the words, but his head was too hazy to offer anything but cooperation. He went where he was pointed, and hoped the instructions were easy to follow.

CHAPTER 28

Jeff and Robert moved through the deck, drawing in the undead with the lure of blood and fresh meat. Jeff assumed control of the fire axe, and much to Sofa's revulsion, used it to dissect several victims of the dead.

Dead or not, they were still people, and there was a difference now. Watching their bodies get cut up and used as bait for an undead fishing trip was more than she was willing to accept. Yet she walked with them, disgusted but not stupid enough to forget about safety being found in numbers.

By the time they reached the elevators, they had herded a group of around fifty second-lifers, each one following the trail of raw meat that was left for them.

They filled each of the elevators with offerings. One by one, the dead were distracted by the squishy delicacies and herded themselves into the elevators. Giving the signal, Jeff and Sofia ran along each one and pressed the buttons to send the cars down to the tenth floor. Only one creature turned around and made a fresh attack on the group, and it was quickly dismembered for its efforts.

"What now?" Sofia asked as she wiped a string of zombie guts from her shoulder.

"Now we distract out visitors," Jeff said. He was out of breath, and almost as pale as Robert. He bled from several deep wounds to his arms and one on his hairline.

Robert fell to the floor, slouched over. His energy was gone.

"You hang in there. I'll be right back," Sofia said, crouching down, placing her head against Robert's.

Jeff headed down the one stairwell while Sofia took the other. They moved into the hallway and waited. As planned, they came out on either side of the group of mercenaries. The formation was ready for them, and both narrowly missed being cut in half by a burst of fire from the M16s each man carried.

The distraction was all they needed, though, because when all four doors opened, the men opened fire. The first wave of the undead swallowed the volley of bullets, but the others pushed through and overtook the group in a flood. Weapons fired and body parts exploded in the air, but the weight of the dead in such tight space meant they were easily overpowered.

The men fought, their armour protecting them from the main onslaught, but with their ranks broken and their weapons removed, the men fell one at a time.

The fight was only over, however, when a grenade rolled from within the mass. It was covered in blood, but Jeff saw it and took his chance. He ran from the stairwell, pulled the pin and gently lobbed the thing back into the group.

"Grenade," he roared the warning to Sofia, who saw him make the move and turned to run back up the stairs.

The explosion rocked the ship, and the floor of the eleventh deck shook and buckled from the initial force of the explosion, and the resulting secondary blasts as the remaining grenades went off.

"We need to move, now," Jeff said as the floor beneath them continued to rumble.

"I'm not leaving him," Sofia said, looking over to Robert, who was slumped even farther over on the floor.

"He's not going to make it." Jeff was realistic. They didn't have the time for such luxuries such as sentimentality.

"Fuck you; he saved my life," Sofia snarled, running over the shaking floor to where Robert sat.

"Robert, Robert, come on, we need to leave." Sofia tugged on his arm, but Robert was nothing but dead weight.

"No," Robert wheezed. "No, get out of here." His voice was barely a whisper.

"I'm not going to leave you here," Sofia said, tears once again filling her eyes.

"Yes, you are. Because I'm dying, and you're just starting to live." Robert forced a smile onto his lips. "It's fine, I'm ready. I was a very angry man, for a very long time. I lost my job, I lost my wife, and before it all, I lost my baby girl. But you know what? I'm not angry anymore. I'm ready to see my baby again."

Sofia didn't get the chance to say anything more. Robert fell silent, falling to one side, and a few moments later, fell through the floor and into the fire and smoke of the deck below.

Sofia ran as the floor fell away beneath her. Jeff was waiting, and together they ran through the deck and back into the open air.

The sun was now rising higher in the sky, the faint glow of the new day's caress now an orange orb, rising up to fight back against the night.

The silence on the deck was deafening. The stench of blood was overpowering, mixed with the salty air of the sea.

"We need to get to the lifeboats," Jeff spoke, yet didn't move.

He stood still for a moment, taking in the extent of the damage wrought on the ship. Moving to the new boat should have signalled the new start Jeff had been longing for. A chance to get away and rebuild himself. Fighting off the apocalypse was not what he had in mind.

"Help me," a fragile voice called out.

Jeff looked around, but couldn't pick any individual out of the masses.

"Where are you?" Sofia called back.

"Hello?" the voice came again, and Jeff found a direction.

"Behind the bar," he said to Sofia, pointing at the decimated structure that had, at one point in time, been the Sun Bar.

They found the survivors huddle together, a woman, two children and an older man. The perfect family, except that each of them were strangers.

"It's ok, come with us," Sofia said, leaning over to help the children to their feet. They could not have been in the double digits in terms of age, yet seemed to be coping with everything better than the adults.

"We need to move to a lifeboat, now," Jeff said, trying hard to keep his voice calm.

They moved on a little way, picking their path around the body-filled pool. Jeff took Sofia by the arm and pulled her to one side. "They are going to blow this boat out of the water." He kept his voice low.

In the Jacuzzi next to them, Jeff could not take his eyes away from the severed head that bounced away on the bubbling jets.

"Who are these people?"

"Terrorists, I don't know. But we need to get these people off the boat. If there is anybody else left, then they will see us and can follow."

"There have to be other survivors." Sofia spoke louder than intended. The people they just picked up turned to stare at them.

"I hope so. But those guys back there, they were professionals. There would be very few people left below us, and I've seen a fuck ton of those dead fuckers walking around."

Sofia said nothing. She nodded at Jeff and walked back to the four new faces.

They found the lifeboat and Jeff reassured everybody he knew how to work the winch that would lower them down to the ocean.

With everybody in the boat, Jeff activated the lifeboat and took his seat.

The descent down the side of the ship seemed to take forever. They all watched in silence as floor after floor passed them by. There were no signs of life. The boat was so filled with blood that it overflowed the deck in places, smearing its way down the side. It looked as if the boat itself was weeping.

They made it to the ocean and detached from the winch. The lifeboats had a simple steering system built in, and they soon moved away from the ship and towards the hazy, dawn-cast shadow of land.

"We made it. We really made it off the ship," the young woman they rescued spoke, weeping as she threw her arms around both Jeff and Sofia.

"We're not out of the woods yet," Jeff said, dashing all of their hopes. "Listen."

They all fell silent, and could easily make out the sound of the rotors starting up.

The helo took to the sky, rising from behind the boat before turning and heading in their direction.

The mounted guns roared back into the life and cut a line of death through the water toward them. Jeff tried to steer the craft out of the way, but it would not react.

"Shit on a fucking stick," he growled, slapping the life raft before catching the eye of the children. "Sorry."

"Look, boats," the young boy announced, sprinting to his feet and pointing toward the horizon.

"It's the Coast Guard," Sofia remarked, squinting into the morning sun. "We are saved."

The approaching helicopter swerved out of the way as the three coastguard ships opened fire. They were small vessels, but well-armed, because the helo showed no interest in continuing the fight. It rose sharply and disappeared out to sea.

The six people on the life raft turned and cheered, only to be thrown through the sea as the *Ocean Princess* exploded.

The explosion took place under water, containing much of the blast, but the surging swell of water was enough to throw the life raft around like a toy in a bathtub.

CHAPTER 29

Captain Yossi Ben Haim watched the life raft rise and fly over the water, but he remained on his intended course. The helicopter had gone, but he knew better than to accept that for fact.

"Keep the guns online. If that thing comes back, I want it blown out of the sky," he ordered, trusting his crew to get the job done.

"Captain, we have reports of four life rafts, two closer to the shore and one further adrift," the voice of Lieutenant Karim Ibarra came through the radio.

"Very good, let's split up. Stay alert. If they blew up the whole ship, who knows what other surprises they have for us." Yossi steered his ship around and brought it alongside the first life raft.

There were six people on board, and he wanted to make sure he was on the deck to greet them.

"You have control of the bridge," he said to his XO.

"Yes, sir," the man answered, moving into position.

Yossi hurried down to the deck, and was just in time to offer his hand to Jeff. "Welcome, my friend. My name is Captain Yossi Ben Haim, and you are safe now." He looked from Jeff to Sofia and over to the others, who stood huddled together beneath a large blanket.

"We will get you medical attention as soon as we get to shore. My two other boats are collecting the others. You are very lucky to have survived, and I know there are lots of people waiting to ask a great many questions once you are patched up."

"That's fine. My name is Jeff Wilcox. I was the XO on the *Princess*. I can answer any questions you have." Jeff winced as he stood up straight.

"You said there were other survivors?" Sofia asked, picking up on what the captain said.

"Yes, four boats in total have been located. They have a built-in distress beacons. Once they are in the water, the beacon activates. But come. We will get you inside and we will be safe in no time." Captain Yossi ushered the six figures inside, and made sure they were comfortable.

His friendly demeanour put them all at ease.

The boat was turned around and their course set for the mainland, the dawn of a new day to the left and the sinking wreckage of their luxury holiday located to the right.

"I'm sorry about your boyfriend," Jeff whispered to Sofia.

She had fallen silent since they started their journey back, and kept her gaze fixed on the sinking ship.

"He was my husband, but thank you. He was the love of my life, but it was not just him. It was everybody, everything. Robert, he saved us, too, and, he didn't deserve to die like that." Sofia turned to look at Jeff, her eyes burning red with tears.

"I know, nobody deserved what happened on that ship, but it is over now. We survived." Jeff put his arms around Sofia's shoulders.

They finished the trip in silence, holding each other. When the ship reached the beach and everybody started to climb down into the shallow surf, Jeff paused. He was not a devout religious man, but he took one final look at the *Ocean Princess*, which had all but disappeared from view, and he said a silent prayer for those they left behind.

Climbing down from the boat, he saw the team of medics that stood waiting for them. Ambulances, fire engines and police cars stood on the sand or the road behind, their lights flaring. Helicopters flew overhead as the search and rescue mission got underway. There was even a small fleet of boats heading out on the water. It was a large effort. Jeff hoped they would not find anything. The dead needed to stay dead.

Everything was peaceful before Sofia's scream shattered the morning air. She had wandered away from the group, something having caught her eye.

Jeff looked up and saw what it was. One of the life rafts from the *Ocean Princess*. The occupants had made it to the shore.

Jeff looked for Captain Ben Haim. The man was staring at him. "We only found three of the life rafts. This must be the fourth," he spoke honestly.

Jeff was running before he knew it. He reached Sofia's side before the rest of the rescue workers. She was stiff as a board, and with good reason.

The life raft was not empty. Two bodies lay in the bottom, floating in a contained ocean of blood and half eaten entrails.

The first paramedics who reached the boat both doubled over and vomited into the ocean at the sight.

"Look," Sofia said, pointing.

Jeff saw it immediately, a path of bloody footprints snaking their way up the beach, outlining the stumbling, haphazard gait of the dead.

Turning toward Captain Ben Haim, Jeff opened his mouth to warn them all when the first scream rang out.

THE END

 SEVERED**PRESS**

f facebook.com/severedpress
twitter.com/severedpress

CHECK OUT OTHER GREAT ZOMBIE NOVELS

900 MILES
by S. Johnathan Davis

John is a killer, but that wasn't his day job before the Apocalypse.
In a harrowing 900 mile race against time to get to his wife just as the dead begin to rise, John, a business man trapped in New York, soon learns that the zombies are the least of his worries, as he sees first-hand the horror of what man is capable of with no rules, no consequences and death at every turn.
Teaming up with an ex-army pilot named Kyle, they escape New York only to stumble across a man who says that he has the key to a rumored underground stronghold called Avalon..... Will they find safety? Will they make it to Johns wife before it's too late?
Get ready to follow John and Kyle in this fast paced thriller that mixes zombie horror with gladiator style arena action!

WHITE FLAG OF THE DEAD
by Joseph Talluto

Millions died when the Enillo Virus swept the earth. Millions more were lost when the victims of the plague refused to stay dead, instead rising to slaughter and feed on those left alive. For survivors like John Talon and his son Jake, they are faced with a choice: Do they submit to the dead, raising the white flag of surrender? Or do they find the will to fight, to try and hang on to the last shreds or humanity?

 SEVEREDPRESS

 facebook.com/severedpress
 twitter.com/severedpress

CHECK OUT OTHER GREAT ZOMBIE NOVELS

RUN
by Rich Restucci

The dead have risen, and they are hungry.

Slow and plodding, they are Legion. The undead hunt the living. Stop and they will catch you. Hide and they will find you. If you have a heartbeat you do the only thing you can: You run.

Survivors escape to an island stronghold: A cop and his daughter, a computer nerd, a garbage man with a piece of rebar, and an escapee from a mental hospital with a life-saving secret. After reaching Alcatraz, the ever expanding group of survivors realize that the infected are not the only threat.

Caught between the viciousness of the undead, and the heartlessness of the living, what choice is there? Run.

THE DEAD WALK THE EARTH
by Luke Duffy

As the flames of war threaten to engulf the globe, a new threat emerges.

A 'deadly flu', the like of which no one has ever seen or imagined, relentlessly spreads, gripping the world by the throat and slowly squeezing the life from humanity.

Eight soldiers, accustomed to operating below the radar, carrying out the dirty work of a modern democracy, become trapped within the carnage of a new and terrifying world.

Deniable and completely expendable. That is how their government considers them, and as the dead begin to walk, Stan and his men must fight to survive.

 SEVERED**PRESS**

 facebook.com/severedpress
 twitter.com/severedpress

CHECK OUT OTHER GREAT ZOMBIE NOVELS

DEAD PULSE RISING
by K. Michael Gibson

Slavering hordes of the walking dead rule the streets of Baltimore, their decaying forms shambling across the ruined city, voracious and unstoppable. The remaining survivors hide desperately, for all hope seems lost... until an armored fortress on wheels plows through the ghouls, crushing bones and decayed flesh. The vehicle stops and two men emerge from its doors, armed to the teeth and ready to cancel the apocalypse.

TOWER OF THE DEAD
by J.V. Roberts

Markus is a hardworking man that just wants a better life for his family. But when a virus sweeps through the halls of his high-rise apartment complex, those plans are put on hold. Trapped on the sixteenth floor with no hope of rescue, Markus must fight his way down to safety with his wife and young daughter in tow.

Floor by bloody floor they must battle through hordes of the hungry dead on a terrifying mission to survive the TOWER OF THE DEAD.

 SEVERED**PRESS**

 facebook.com/severedpress
 twitter.com/severedpress

CHECK OUT OTHER GREAT ZOMBIE NOVELS

DEAD ASCENT
by Jason McPhearson

The dead have risen and they are hungry...

Grizzled war veteran turned game warden, Brayden James and a small group of survivors, fight their way through the rugged wilderness of southern Appalachia to an isolated cabin in the hope of finding sanctuary. Every terrifying step they make they are stalked by a growing mass of staggering corpses, and a raging forest fire, set by the government in hopes of containing the virus.

As all logical routes off the mountain are cut off from them, they seek the higher ground, but they soon realize there is little hope of escape when the dead walk and the world burns.

CHAOS THEORY
by Rich Restucci

The world has fallen to a relentless enemy beyond reason or mercy. With no remorse they rend the planet with tooth and nail.

One man stands against the scourge of death that consumes all.

Teamed with a genius survivalist and a teenage girl, he must flee the teeming dead, the evils of humans left unchecked, and those that would seek to use him. His best weapon to stave off the horrors of this new world? His wit.

www.ingramcontent.com/pod-product-compliance
Lightning Source LLC
Chambersburg PA
CBHW020309150626
46552CB00022B/2232